BOOKS BY PATRICK SAMPHIRE

The Mennik Thorn Novels

Shadow of a Dead God

Nectar for the God

Strange Cargo

Legacy of a Hated God

The Casebook of Harriet George Series

The Dinosaur Hunters

A Spy in the Deep

The Secrets of the Dragon Tomb Series

(for children)

Secrets of the Dragon Tomb

The Emperor of Mars

Short Story Collection

At the Gates and Other Stories

STRANGE CARGO

A MENNIK THORN SHORT NOVEL (BOOK 3)

PATRICK SAMPHIRE

FIVE FATHOMS PRESS

For my brother, Martin Samphire.
Just checking that you're still reading these.

AUTHOR'S NOTE

STRANGE CARGO IS A SHORT NOVEL.

It's a bit under half the length of a normal Mennik Thorn novel. Some of you may be wondering why I chose to make the third Mennik Thorn novel shorter than the others. The truth is, I hadn't originally planned to write this as a separate book at all. Some of the events here had originally been planned to fit in Nectar for the God, the second book in the series. But it quickly became apparent that that wasn't going to work.

These novels are carefully constructed, and to work, the disparate plot strands have to weave carefully together and link at the end. If I have too many of them, the books will lose focus and drift. But there was one particular plot strand in *Nectar for the God* that didn't get fully resolved in a way that satisfied me. I considered moving it to the next (and final) book in the series, *Legacy of a Hated God*. But again that hit the same problem. *Legacy* is already going to be a complex book with lots of big events, plot strands, and character developments to draw together. Plugging in more strands would make it lose shape.

So, you've ended up with an extra, if somewhat shorter Mennik Thorn novel. I hope you'll enjoy getting this extra, unplanned visit to Nik's world. Things, as you might expect, are about to go bad for him...

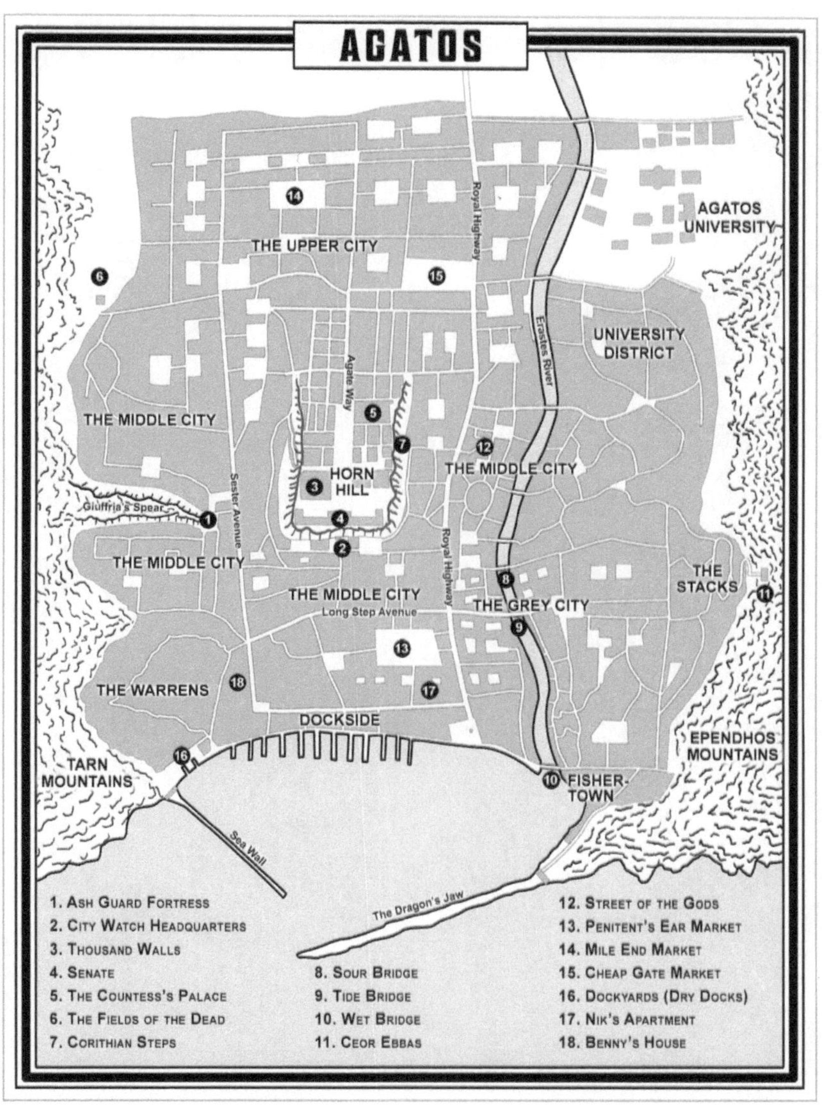

The city of Agatos.
To see a full-size map, visit:
patricksamphire.com/agatos-map-3

THE STORY SO FAR

KEY CONCEPTS

Agatos – A large city at the mouth of the Erastes River, looking out onto the Erastes Bay and the Yttradian Sea beyond. Agatos is a trading city situated at the beginning of the Lidharan Highway, which carries most trade to the cities of the north. The city is theoretically ruled by the Senate, but the city's high mages and the Ash Guard also hold significant power and influence.

The Gods – Many gods, alive, dead, and of indeterminate status, are worshipped in Agatos, although they rarely bother lending their power to their worshippers. You can find a list of the gods mentioned in the Mennik Thorn books in Appendix 2.

Magic – When gods die, their mortal remains begin to rot. The effluent from this permeates the air, the water, and the earth anywhere they were worshipped, being particularly intense where their remains are found. This effluent is the raw magic that mages draw on to shape into spells. They try not to talk about the origin of their power too often.

The Ash Guard – A martial order who use the ashes of the dead sun god, Sharshak, to neutralise all forms of magic and even the power of most gods. They rigorously police the actions of mages, supernatural entities, and gods that step out of line.

MAIN CHARACTERS

Mennik (Nik) Thorn, our protagonist – A minor mage who has set himself up as a freelance operator in the poorer parts of Agatos, having walked away from the machinations and corruption of the high mages, particularly those of the Countess, his estranged mother.

Benyon (Benny) Field – Nik's best friend since childhood, although they have recently fallen out over Nik putting Benny's daughter, Sereh, in danger. Benny is an unapologetic thief governed by a complicated and unbreakable code of favours and debts.

Sereh Field – Benny's daughter. A terrifying 11-year-old far too competent and dangerous with a knife and with the apparent ability to move undetected through shadows. Nik thinks she is probably one of the most dangerous people in the city, although Benny sees her as vulnerable and in need of protection.

Mica Coldrock, formerly **Mica Thorn** – Nik's younger half-sister, a powerful mage who has maintained a relationship with their mother.

Jettuk Kehsereen – A scholar from the city of Khorasan now living in Agatos. He and Nik worked together to rescue Kehsereen's nephew from the god of nightmares, Enabgal. Now Kehsereen's nephew is in the protective care of the Ash Guard, whose Ash suppresses the boy's out-of-control natural magical abilities.

Captain Meroi Gale – A captain of the Ash Guard. Nik has an unrequited crush on Captain Gale and works casually for her as an informant. He has yet to gather the courage to ask her out on a date.

Elosyn and Holera Brook – Two of Nik's most tolerant friends. A married couple. Elosyn works as a baker at Nuil's Coffee House, and Holera is a chef at her own restaurant. Both have been known to feed Nik when his business is doing particularly badly and patch him up when he's been injured. Which happens far more often than it should.

The Countess, Senator Anatase Coldrock formerly **Solone Thorn** – Nik's estranged mother. A high mage controlling much of the Senate.

The Wren – A high mage controlling crime in the lower parts of Agatos.

Melecho Kael – The Wren's bodyguard / enforcer / assistant / gardener.

Squint – An information broker working for the Wren out of Dumonoc's bar.

Dumonoc – The world's must unwelcoming barman.

Scholar Longstream – a scholar at Agatos University to whom Nik turned for help in SHADOW OF A DEAD GOD, but who refused all assistance unless Nik would raise the body of the founder of Agatos, **Agate Blackspear**, known as the **Godkiller**, the city's first high mage. Nik refused, as a point of principle.

RECENT EVENTS

In SHADOW OF A DEAD GOD, Nik Thorn is a second-rate mage, just about getting by, keeping his head down, drinking at Dumonoc's bar, and taking on small jobs that require magic, such as breaking curses, spying on cheating spouses, finding lost pets, and hunting ghosts. That all changes when he agrees to help Benny steal a ledger from the high mage, Carnelian Silkstar, and they find themselves framed for a brutal, magical murder they didn't commit.

As Nik desperately tries to prove their innocence, more murders seem to follow him around, each of them apparently committed by an impossible ghost-beast.

Eventually, Nik tracks the origin of these attacks to a powerful mage, Enne Lowriver, who supposedly works for the Countess, but who is in fact the secret leader of a cult of the dead beast god, Ah'té. Nik, Benny, and Sereh manage to disrupt Lowriver's attempted resurrection of the beast god and injure Lowriver, who is eventually killed by Captain Gale. In the process, Benny swallows the relic that summoned the ghost of the beast god, a claw. Nik, meanwhile, has incurred a debt to the criminal high mage, the Wren.

In NECTAR FOR THE GOD, Nik's attempts to dodge the debt he owes to the Wren finally fail and he is forced to infiltrate his mother's court to obtain information the Wren can use against the Countess in their ongoing feud. At the same time, he is employed by a widower, Mr. Mirian, whose wife murdered a stranger in public and then killed herself. Mr. Mirian wants Nik to prove that his wife was under magical influence.

As Nik follows the clues, he finds the murder victim's closest friends being killed, too, by a force that seems to have command of astonishing magical power and the ability to take over bystanders. During his investigation, he encounters a scholar, Jettuk Kehsereen, who is searching for his nephew who went missing weeks earlier and who appears to have a link to the murder victims, and also manages to fall foul of a vicious smuggling gang. All in a day's work.

Nik and Kehsereen discover that the victims have been feeding natural mages to the until-now lost god of nightmares in exchange for success. But those victims made a mistake by trying to feed the god a natural high mage whose power is too great to contain and who, in his madness, has been lashing out and killing them. Nik rescues the boy – Kehsereen's nephew – from the god and turns the god over to the Ash Guard.

The other half of his quest hasn't gone so well, though. Nik was traumatised by his experience growing up with his mother's impossibly high standards and her obvious contempt for him. When he puts off his job for the Wren too long, Benny and Sereh's lives are put at risk, leading to a rift between them. Benny has been Nik's best friend since child, but now he wants nothing to do with him. The loss hits Nik hard, and he knows it's his fault.

Nik finally hands over the information the Wren wanted, only to discover that, without his knowledge, he has been used by his mother, once again, as no more than a tool in her own schemes.

Now read on...

CHAPTER ONE

YOU DIDN'T NEED TO BE A CITIZEN OF AGATOS TO LEARN ONE very simple rule: never threaten a mage with a gun.

If you were lucky, the gun just wouldn't fire. The flint would jam before hitting the steel, or the powder would be inexplicably damp, or your finger wouldn't move on the trigger.

If you were unlucky, the barrel might block itself and the gun would explode, taking half your face with it.

Like I said, not a great idea.

Threatening a mage with a couple of dozen guns, on the other hand, well, that was where things got more tricky.

I'd had a long day. A market trader in the Penitent's Ear had thought her husband was cheating on her, so I'd spent the last few days following the bastard everywhere. It was the hottest part of the summer, and most sensible people kept indoors for most of the day. But this bloke pushed a delivery cart back and forth between the docks, the market, and various businesses around the city, and I had trudged along behind him like the idiot I was. It had been sweaty and exhausting, and she hadn't needed a mage to do it. Her husband certainly wasn't using magical means to hide his activities. But since I had sworn off any jobs that might even tangentially involve gods or mages, I couldn't afford to be fussy.

As it turned out, he wasn't cheating on her. Not with another woman or another man, anyway. He was cheating on her with a bar and a whole bunch of drinks. He would tell her he had a job to do, then he would head for the bar, where he would drink alone for several hours at a time. I had reported my findings to my client this evening, and hadn't that gone well? She would have been happier if I had told her he was screwing a stranger. Luckily, these days I took payment upfront.

After that, all I'd wanted was to get back home, fall over, and sleep for several days.

Which was why it came as an unpleasant surprise when I turned onto Corrastar Street, with my apartment and office in sight, and two dozen men and women, all armed with muskets, stepped out of the shadows and levelled their weapons at me.

Of course, jamming a gun wasn't the only mage trick I had up my sweaty sleeves. I could cast a shield around myself or send out a burst of magical energy to knock them flying. But that was a lot of lead for my shield to catch, and I had never tried to knock this many people senseless in one go. I had the horrible, gnawing suspicion that whichever way this played out, I would end up with a lot more holes in me than I had started with.

I knew I pissed people off, but this was quite a lot of people to have pissed off in one go. I didn't think I even knew this many people.

I straightened, hefted my mage's rod, forced a smile, and prepared to duck.

The lower parts of Agatos – the Warrens, Dockside, Fishertown – weren't known for their respectability. These were the places you ended up when the city took one look at you and told you to fuck right back off. Even my apartment, just a couple of streets away from the Penitent's Ear market and theoretically within the Middle City, was the kind of place that respectable citizens avoided if they possibly could. But even by the standards of the lower city, this lot would be kicked out of most bars and inns. Hard, wind-burned faces fixed on me with a cold professionalism. Yeah, these weren't people I wanted to fuck with. Shame they seemed to want to fuck with me.

The evening air was still hot; even in the dead of night it never really grew cold at this time of year. That was why I was sweating, absolutely not because of all those gun barrels pointed directly at me.

As always when I was nervous, I opened my mouth. "Is that a bit of overcompensation there, boys, or are you just happy to see me?"

All right, it wasn't my best line, but you try better when enough people to start a small riot are lining up to shoot you. Anyway, all it got was frowns. I was just about to explain that I had been insulting their manhoods – again, probably ineffective when half of them weren't male – when someone stepped up behind me, pulled a sack over my head, and smacked me across the back of my skull.

It was, I thought as blackness claimed me, like getting back to the good old days.

When I woke, I still had the sack over my head and my hands were tied behind my back. I was lying somewhere hard and damp. Almost chilly, too. So, either somewhere magically cooled or underground. I didn't like either option. Magic would mean one of the powers in Agatos had taken an interest in me again, and that never ended well. Underground ... well, I'd had my fill of underground. I'd sworn off the tunnels and ruins beneath the city as thoroughly as I'd sworn off the docks and the ocean beyond. And, yeah, I did realise that at this rate I would be running out of city to live in.

It was dark outside the sack, as well. If there was someone else out there, more fool them, because it wasn't like I could have seen them through the sack, anyway.

This wasn't the first time I had woken tied hand and foot. For some reason, people seemed to enjoy knocking me unconscious. Some of them didn't even know me. The last time it had happened, I had been mistakenly drugged and lost control of my powers. As far as mistakes went, it put some of my own into proportion. As far as I knew, Jettuk Kehsereen, the man who had drugged me then, was the only one who knew about the ulu-aru drug that stole magical powers, but I pulled in a little raw magic to check. Yep. At least that was working. I would be able to burn my way out of these ropes if I needed to. Of course, if all those bastards with their guns were still around, that might not be the greatest idea.

Fuck it. I was a mage of Agatos. Not a great one, admittedly, not even an adequate one, really, but I wasn't helpless, and I wasn't comfortable. I focused my magic and cut through the ropes holding me. I even managed to avoid cutting my own wrists by accident. I was getting better at this gig.

I sat up and pulled off the sack.

As I did so, someone sparked a lamp into light.

I was in a big room, no windows. Underground, as I had guessed. Maybe a cellar. Several large barrels stood against the back wall. The air was still and, frankly, pretty nasty, which was no doubt caused by the great crowd of armed men and women forming a semicircle around me.

They had been standing there in the dark after all. Twats.

"You know you could have just bought me a beer, right?"

There I went. Spouting my mouth off again. I was yet to find a circumstance where that made things better.

Someone I hadn't at first noticed stepped through the crowd and stood over me, hands on her hips.

Oh. Oh shit. Now I remembered who these guys were.

Several weeks back, during an investigation, I had accidentally charged into a smugglers' lair at an inn called *The Bloody End*, smashed the place up, given a good dozen smugglers a magical kicking, then fled through their secret stash of smuggled goods. They had been pretty pissed off, and they had come after me. Eventually, they had been scared off by the Wren's people, who had also been pissed off with me. That was a pretty good encapsulation of how my life had been going this last month or two. That, and gods and mages trying to kill me.

I should have known the smugglers hadn't forgotten.

The Mycedan woman standing in front of me had been in *The Bloody End* that evening, and as luck would have it, she seemed to be the head of the whole damned smuggling gang.

Her clothes were colourful but patched, and the jewellery around her neck and wrists was showy, if not particularly valuable. Having Benny as a friend meant I had become a minor expert on the value of jewellery. (A typical conversation would go, Benny: "Take a look at this, mate." Me: "For fuck's sake, put that away before someone sees it." Benny: "Nice, innit? Worth a good bit. It was just lying about, if you can believe it." Me: "In someone else's house." Benny: "Well, I'm hardly going to nick it from my own house, am I?")

Having *had* Benny as a friend, I should say. I still hadn't healed that rift. Not that I hadn't tried. I had called around a dozen times, but he hadn't answered, and I was too wary of Sereh's booby traps to let myself in to confront him.

There would be time to worry about that if my new

friends here didn't cut off my hands and nail my head to a wall.

"Nice place," I said. "Not so impressed by the lighting, though. A bit ... intermittent."

The woman's expression didn't change as she looked down on me. She would have to do better than that. I had been glared at by some of the most dangerous and powerful people in Agatos. I smiled back, trying to look serene. Some people have said it makes me look like I have a hot poker shoved up my arse, but those people are no longer talking to me, so...

"You lost us our mage," the woman said at last. She still hadn't introduced herself, and I had a feeling she wasn't going to. Kind of rude, but not as rude as the kidnapping and threatening me, I supposed.

"He was fine when I left him. A bit of a bruised head, I reckon, but nothing permanent." And he had started it. He had thrown magic at me, so I had hit him over the back of the head with a bottle. I hadn't been gentle, but we mages healed quickly.

"And then your Ash Guard came around, and he was on the next ship out of here."

Ah. Yeah. I had told Captain Gale about him.

"You owe us," the woman said.

"I don't think so." They had been trying to kill me. I had a right to defend myself. I made a move to rise, and all the muskets came up. I sat again. "On the other hand..." I forced my smile wider. "What exactly was it you wanted me to do?"

The leader of the smugglers made a gesture, and the muskets lowered. I always felt a bit better when a couple of dozen people weren't pointing guns at me.

"We have an important shipment arriving in four days. You're going to make sure it arrives safely and no one notices it being unloaded."

"That's all, is it?" That had been sarcasm. I wasn't sure she picked it up

"It's what our last mage did for us. Before you fucked that up."

Right. And if he could hide a whole ship from sight, he had been a lot more powerful than I'd realised, and I had been lucky to come away from it with all my limbs attached. I suppressed a shudder.

Not that I had to hide the whole ship. Ships sailed into and out of the port all day, every day. The smugglers' ship would come in at night, no doubt. All I would have to do was keep away any prying eyes until it was unloaded, then come the morning, the customs agents could poke around to their little hearts' delight. I had a few tricks up my sleeve that might do the job. I could pull it off. It had to be a better option than being murdered in a damp cellar.

"I don't suppose I'll be getting your mage's pay, too?" I said. When the woman didn't answer, I added, "So, what are you bringing in?"

"That's none of your business, is it?"

And there was the rub. I didn't care about most of the things smugglers snuck in. If they wanted to dodge import taxes on coffee or tea or spices or silks, I couldn't give a fuck. It wasn't like those taxes would find their way to helping the poorer parts of Agatos. But what if that wasn't what they were bringing in? What if it was something dangerous? Innocent people could get hurt. I didn't want that on my conscience.

"The more you tell me, the better I can make sure you get in clear." Like I cared if they did. If I had my way, the customs agents and the Watch could bang the lot of them up.

The smuggler's face didn't crack. I wasn't getting an inch out of her. "All you need to know is that you'll join the ship at midnight in four days' time. There will be a small boat waiting near the end of the Dragon's Jaw to carry you out there. The ship will unload at the dockyards. It'll take half an hour at most. You will make sure no one sees a thing."

The dockyards occupied the western end of the harbour, past where the wharfs and warehouses ended. Agatos didn't build ships, but the Yttradian Sea could be harsh, and plenty of arriving vessels needed work. They could be brought out of the water at the dockyards, planks replaced and re-caulked, tillers and masts repaired, cracked keels mended, or whatever the fuck else needed doing. I was hardly an expert, and I didn't want to be. Me and the ocean didn't get along.

The prying eyes the smugglers were worried about wouldn't be the dockyard guards or the City Watch, who would have been paid off, nor the customs officials, who would be tucked up nicely in their beds. The smugglers' real problem would be that the dockyards abutted the Warrens, and the assorted scallywags and scumballs – my childhood peers, in other words – who prowled the streets looking for a mark would have their eyes on any ship that came in. I doubted they would try to take on a notorious smuggling gang, but information was currency here, and there were people in this city who would. My job, it seemed, would be to make sure that information never seeped out.

"You should know," the woman said, "that if you betray us, if you fail us, I will feed your balls to a dog. And after that, your day will get very, very bad."

CHAPTER TWO

THEY DID THE WHOLE SACK-OVER-THE-HEAD THING AGAIN ON the way out, as well as the tied hands, and dumped me in the narrow street not far from my apartment. I freed myself, ignored the amused glances, jeers, and pointing fingers of passers-by, straightened my shirt, and made my way back to my apartment with as much dignity as I could manage.

I had converted the front room into a makeshift office and left it free from wards. It was never a good idea to fry potential clients before you had decided whether you wanted to take their cases. I did keep the door locked when I wasn't there, though – I didn't have much worth stealing, but I liked having a chair to sit on and a desk between me and my clients. Sometimes people got angry, and a desk made a decent barrier.

The man who was sitting on my front step was

someone I had seen hundreds of times over the last five years, but context was everything, and it was only when he spoke that I made the connection.

"Where the fuck have you been all night?" he grunted.

"Dumonoc?" What in the dark, sunken Depths was my least favourite bartender doing here?

"Who the fuck did you think it was? Your aunt?"

"I don't have an aunt." I stepped past him and unlocked the door. I could do that with magic, but the key was easier. That was something a lot of mages didn't understand. Magic wasn't always the best option. "What do you want, Dumonoc?"

"I've got a job for you." He stood.

"What's happened? Lost your last customers? Because I've got to tell you, it'll take more than magic to get people back in there."

"Never stopped you."

"Yeah, well, I'm cheap."

He followed me in. I walked around the desk and took my seat, indicating the other chair. My mage light had come on as we entered. I was proud of that. It was a far harder spell than it sounded, setting a magical light to appear whenever anyone came into a room. It had taken a lot of fine-tuning. I was thinking of selling it. The light was a lot warmer and less sickly than the morgue-lamps that illuminated much of the city, and it ran off the raw magic that permeated every part of Agatos. But it had been a lot of work, and I didn't know if it was worth my while.

I had never seen Dumonoc in the full light before. His

bar was notoriously dark and dingy. He looked older and paler than I had thought, and if possible, even more grumpy, although that might just have been because he'd had to come to me for help. I had that effect on people.

He chewed his lip for a while, then raised his head to meet my eyes. "I think someone has cursed my drinks."

My eyebrows shot up, and I wasn't even putting it on. "Really? How could you tell the difference?" Dumonoc's drinks had a reputation. If they didn't dissolve your teeth and erode your stomach lining faster than acid poured on paper, then there was a better than even chance they would poison you. The only thing in their favour was that they were cheap, and people left you alone in his bar.

"Fuck's sake. I didn't want to come here, you know?"

I shrugged and indicated the door. It wasn't like I'd invited the bastard.

His glower intensified. "My husband said I had to."

"I didn't know you were married." The idea of anyone wanting to spend, well, any time at all with Dumonoc was a mystery to me.

"Why the fuck would I tell you?"

Fair point.

The urge to tell Dumonoc to fuck off, and maybe throw a bottle at him on his way out, was almost overwhelming. But I still needed clients, and word got around. Anyway, I quite liked the idea of relieving him of his money. Every silver watchman I squeezed out of him would make up for one of the appalling drinks I had suffered in his bar over the years.

"Tell me what happened."

He grunted again. His favourite form of communication. "This morning when I came in, when I checked the drinks, they had gone off. Every single one of them. The beer, the wine, the spirits. All of them were undrinkable. I even opened a couple of bottles from storage, but they were the same."

"Again. How could you tell the difference?"

Dumonoc lifted his chin. "That shit you and Squint and all the other cheapskates drink isn't the only stuff I have, you know. I have good stuff, too. Not that you would pay for it."

"No one goes there for the drinks." Nor the atmosphere, the conversation, nor, come to think of it, the light, as Dumonoc's bar was always plunged into near-constant darkness.

"You don't. Anyway, I had to go out and buy new wine. It was fine at first, but within a couple of hours, it had gone the same way."

All right. That was strange. I wasn't sure it sounded like a curse. Not on the drinks, anyway, unless someone had been there to curse the new bottles. More like a curse on the whole establishment. And while Dumonoc's unironic habit of insulting his customers didn't make him many friends, it would take someone pretty potent to cast a curse like that. Not necessarily a trained mage, but someone with a good amount of natural magical aptitude.

"Fine. I'll help you." It would drive him crazy to be in my debt. "But not tonight, and it's going to cost you."

~

At this time of year, in the burning, weighted heat of midsummer, you had three choices in Agatos. First, you could be indecently wealthy and fuck off to your summer palace at Carn's Break, where the high, wooded hills provided a pleasantly spring-like climate. If, for whatever reason, you hadn't been hoarding wealth at the expense of the city's poor, or you just couldn't stand the other greedy parasites up there, you were left with the other two options: stay inside during the day with your shutters closed, or just go out anyway like a fool. Like me.

By the time I dragged myself from my tangled sheets, moaned a bit, and staggered out, it was already too hot. They called Agatos 'the White City' exactly for days like this. Most of the buildings had been whitewashed to reflect away the heat, and while that might have helped keep the insides of the buildings cool, it turned the streets into furnaces. I tried to keep to the shadows, but it didn't do much good. By the time I reached Dumonoc's bar, I was soaked in sweat and almost ready to ask for one of his undrinkable drinks.

The place was empty of customers. Whether that was because of the hour or because news had spread that his drinks were even worse than usual, I didn't know. Dumonoc was standing glumly behind the bar, bottles of drink stacked along the wood in front of him.

"What?" I said, as I let the door close behind me. At

least it was cooler down here. “No insults? No telling me to fuck off?”

I could see him grinding his teeth. *Can’t insult me now you need me, can you?*

On the other hand... “You’re a shit customer, you know? You buy the cheapest wine, you don’t tip, and you scare other customers away.”

“Me?”

“No one wants to drink with a mage around. Unsettles them.”

“Yeah, well. You’re a shit barman. Shall we just get on with it?”

“Fine.” Dumonoc indicated around behind the bar. “I carried it all out so you won’t go poking around the back.”

Nice.

The bottles hadn’t just been stacked on the bar and the shelves, but also on the floor, along with half a dozen casks. It must have taken a whole lot of hauling, all so he didn’t have to let me into his poxy storeroom.

“Just... Stand still and don’t say anything,” I said.

I let my eyes unfocus.

Every mage had a different way of sensing magic. For some, it was like music, for others a taste on their tongue. Me, I saw magic as colours and patterns when I unfocused my eyes. The magic that wrapped around the bottles and casks was like a fine, sea-blue net. A fairly common structure for a curse. What wasn’t normal, though, was that the net of magic seemed to be moving organically, like a weird sea creature with too many tentacles sliding over rocks.

Curses were static magic, clamped onto the object or person until they crumbled or someone broke them. I had never seen a curse that seemed restless like this. It covered almost all of the casks and bottles, other than two bottles on the end of the bar. The magic of the curse seemed to stretch towards those two, like questing roots through soil, brushing over them.

"Are they new ones?" I asked, nodding towards them.

"Got them this morning, just before you got here. Have to have something to serve."

He wasn't going to have them for much longer if I was right about this. The curse seemed to be infecting the new bottles. I had never even heard of anything like that.

"I'm going to try to get rid of it," I said. "Um. You might want to stand back."

Curses were delicate things, even if they could have devastating effects. Most would disintegrate over time, but they weren't hard to break, and that breaking was rarely dramatic. But I wasn't sure what I was dealing with here.

I reached out with a scalpel of magic and sliced through a thread of the curse. It was like cutting through the strands of a spider's web. The curse simply crumpled, falling in on itself, and dissipated. It took a few different cuts – it was an extensive curse – but in a minute or two it was gone.

"We're done," I said, blinking my eyes back into focus. Doing that for too long always gave me a headache.

"This lot drinkable again?" Dumonoc nodded at the stacked bottles and casks.

I resisted the urge to say it never had been. There was only so many times a joke was funny. "I doubt it. Your new bottles are probably fine, but you're too late with the rest."

Outrage twisted Dumonoc's face. "What the fuck did I pay you for? Twenty silver shields, and you didn't even save my stock."

This was why I demanded payment upfront. "I saved those two bottles and every other drink you were going to have to buy. I can always put the curse back, if you prefer."

That was a bluff. I had no idea how to construct a curse like that, but Dumonoc didn't need to know.

"You're a bastard, Mennik Thorn."

I shrugged. I'd been called worse, often by Dumonoc himself, and I couldn't perform miracles.

I left him there, staring at his ruined drinks, and headed for the door. I didn't get much gratitude in this job, but I did get paid. That was about all I could hope for.

"And don't you ever fucking come back!" Dumonoc shouted as I headed out the door.

CHAPTER THREE

THE MOST IMPORTANT PRINCIPLE IN RUNNING ANY BUSINESS was to leave the customer happy. Unless that customer was Dumonoc, in which case his tears were my wine. I found myself whistling as I strode across the small plaza in front of his bar. It wasn't often I felt this satisfied at the end of a job.

That satisfaction lasted all the way until I reached the Royal Highway, glanced down towards the docks, and was suddenly reminded of my smuggling friends and what they wanted me to do in just three days' time. Shit like that shouldn't be able to happen. No one should be able to grab you and force you to do whatever they wanted. In a wealthy city like Agatos, there should be protections. And maybe there were for those in the Upper City, the merchants, the politicians, the rich, and the connected. But not down here. Here, people were left on their own. Don't get me wrong. I loved my city, but this I fucking hated, the way everyone crapped on those at the bottom, and no one with the power to change it gave a toss. This shit with the smugglers was just a symptom.

My easiest option would be to go along with their demands, do the job, and get out of there. But I didn't think they would really be done with me after one job. They would just have more leverage the next time they wanted something. I had grown up in the Warrens. I had seen too many people dragged down like that, and I didn't want to join them. I wasn't becoming some smuggling gang's pet mage.

If I refused, though, I would spend the rest of my life looking over my shoulder, waiting for them to come for me again. No one could get lucky forever.

I reckoned that was what the smugglers were relying on. My helplessness, torn between two dirty alternatives. They wanted me to think I had no other choices.

They were wrong. I wasn't helpless. Unlike most people down here, I did have contacts, and I wasn't giving in without a fight.

Agatos was an old city. Towns and cities had occupied the mouth of the Erastes Valley for thousands of years. Before that, there had been scattered settlements, and probably, before *that*, roving bands of hunter-gatherers. Across those millennia, people had worshipped their gods. Despite the claims of various religions, no one knew where gods came from, what exactly they were, nor how they died. But we knew they could die, and when they did, their rotting bodies became the source of raw magic, strongest where those bodies lay, but spreading wherever they had held influence. Over the years, a lot of gods had been worshipped or feared in the Erastes Valley and then had died. As a result, Agatos was lousy with power.

Between mages and the supernatural entities that fed on and manipulated raw magic – and the gods themselves, both living and dead – the potential for magical disaster was enormous. The only reason Agatos still stood and thrived was because of the presence of the Ash Guard, whose Ash – carried in pouches or smeared on their skin – destroyed all types of magic. Any mage with half a brain stayed as far away from the Ash Guard as they could.

And that was the smugglers' first mistake, because it turned out that I wasn't the kind of mage with half a brain. I was a frequent enough visitor to the Guard that I had a contact I could call on: Captain Meroi Gale.

The Ash Guard fortress was built up to and into Giuffria's Spear, a spur of cliff protruding into the western part of the city, walling off the Warrens from the better parts of Agatos. The Ash Guard fortress didn't get a lot of visitors. When you had a reputation as mage-killers, people tended to keep their distance. Heat haze shimmered silver over the empty plaza as I made my way across it. I hammered on the fortress doors, declined the offer to wait inside the Ash-soaked fortress, and stood in the heat of the morning sun until Captain Gale finally appeared.

The captain was a small, muscular woman with the straight black hair and dark olive skin of an Agatos native.

She had also kicked my arse both with and without Ash, which always added a certain excitement to our interactions.

When she saw me waiting, her eyebrows lifted. "I thought things had been a bit peaceful."

I grimaced. This was awkward already.

"I assume you've awoken some ancient, evil god again?"

Oh, come on! That hadn't been me. I'd just happened to be nearby and in the way. Twice. I couldn't tell if she was teasing or serious, so I decided to ignore it. "You remember that smuggling gang I told you about a while back?"

"The one with the mage tossing his power about?"

"Yeah. They're back in business. I got a tip-off about a new operation they're running." That wasn't a lie, as far as it went, and I was quite pleased with the way I had managed to phrase it. "I thought you'd dealt with them."

"I dealt with the mage, Nik. Why? Is he back?"

"No."

"They have a new mage involved?"

Um. Yeah. There was no way I was answering that one truthfully. "I know they're bringing in a cargo. It could be weapons. It could be drugs. It could be something worse. I thought you might want to stop it. You told me to report trouble."

She eyed me, head on one side. It made me squirm. "Magical trouble," she said slowly. "If it's not magic, it's not my jurisdiction. I don't have time to take on things that are none of my business." She looked up at me through steady, brown eyes. "Because if there's one thing I can tell you for sure, it's that somewhere out there some mage is cooking up a stupid scheme that I am going to have to deal with before someone gets hurt." She raised her eyebrows meaningfully. "Are they bringing in something magical?"

I grimaced again. "I don't know."

"Then even if I wanted to help, I can't. There are good reasons the Ash Guard aren't allowed to interfere in non-magical affairs. If you put your mind to it, I'm sure you can figure out why."

Yeah. I could. I just didn't want to. But I got the hint. I raised my hands in surrender.

"Look, Nik. If you do have information, you should take it to the City Watch."

That wasn't going to happen. Even if they hadn't been bribed, I would sooner slam my nuts in a door. The City Watch hated my guts. They suspected – rightly – that I had broken Benny out of gaol a few months back and injured several of their colleagues in the process. I hadn't meant to hurt anyone, and they couldn't do anything about it after Benny and I had received pardons, but I didn't think they would be leaping to my aid.

"Maybe I'll do that," I said.

"You've got good instincts, even if you do cause chaos everywhere you go. Any magical threat, bring it to me, and I'll deal with it. I just can't touch anything else."

"Yeah. All right." I raised a hand in farewell and made my self-conscious way back across the open plaza.

Fuck! So much for my contacts. I was going to have to deal with this one myself.

~

WHENEVER I WANTED TO FIND OUT ABOUT THE CROOKED goings-on in this city – the ones carried out in the lower city, anyway – I had two options. The first was Benny, whose own burglary habit brought him into contact with a whole bunch of crooks and thugs. But Benny wasn't talking to me after I had unintentionally put Sereh in danger and not warned him about it. Yeah, my fault completely, and I didn't blame him for the way he'd reacted.

The second option was Squint, one of the Wren's information brokers. But Squint operated out of Dumonoc's bar, and I reckoned Dumonoc wouldn't exactly be pleased to see me again so soon. Anyway, anything I asked Squint would find its way back to the wrong people by the end of the day.

I sat under the awning of a coffee house on Perlit Avenue from where I could look down to the glittering Erastes Bay, the very un-glittering harbour, and the distinctly foul docks. An ocean breeze cooled the street, if only a little, and carried the faint smell of dead fish heat-baked on the rocks. I sipped an iced, sweet coffee and ran through my options.

Squint wasn't the only information broker in Agatos, but it would take time to build up trust. A bribe might be enough to persuade a customs agent to speak, if they knew anything and if I had the money to spare. Dumonoc's fee had been a good one for a morning's work, but I had rent due soon. I couldn't afford to throw it away on bribes until I was sure I could get something useful.

No, I was going to have to get down and dirty and figure out what the smugglers were up to myself.

I tossed down the rest of my coffee, almost choked on a lump of ice, and rose, before realising that I wasn't going to discover anything at this time of day. I headed back to my office, where I found one of my regular customers, Mr. Inles, waiting.

I didn't even have to ask what he wanted. He had lost his dog. Again. This must make it a dozen times in the last few weeks. I was beginning to suspect Mr. Inles, who lived alone, was simply looking for an excuse for human company.

I spent the rest of the afternoon tracking down his dog. I was getting good at the tracking spell by now. It didn't take long to find his dog around the back of a butcher's shop only a couple of streets from where Mr. Inles lived, but it took a whole lot longer to catch the bloody thing. It had an almost preternatural ability to dodge the net spells I threw at it. I ended up chasing it up and down the street several times before I managed to throw myself on it and get hold of its collar. At least it gave the locals some entertainment, and the dog seemed to enjoy it. I had suggested a leash to Mr. Inles, but he wasn't having it, and anyway, it was the regular customers that kept you in business.

Eventually, evening slipped into darkness as the sun sank behind the western mountains. On the far side of the valley, the eastern mountains were still coated in liquid, blinding gold, but down here in the streets, the shadows had thickened to night. I joined the crowds leaving the shelter of their homes.

The dockyards lay on the far side of the Warrens, almost where the city pressed into the sheer cliffs of the western valley wall. The most sensible route there was along the quay, but that would take me right through the smugglers' territory. So, I cut through the Warrens and almost got lost on the way.

The streets and alleys of the Warrens defied mapping. Old houses crumbled and driftwood shacks sprang up in alleyways. The mudbricks, timbers, and old stones of one house were always reused for another, even more rickety construction. A passageway that led through the maze one month would be blocked the next. I didn't come back to the Warrens enough to keep track of the changes. I had grown up here. It had shaped me, and it still ran through me. But I didn't know it anymore. Maybe that was why I normally kept away.

It took me several wrong turns before I finally found my way out in sight of the dockyards.

I was certain the smuggling gang would have moved their base from *The Bloody End* after Captain Gale's visit, and I reckoned that if they were bringing in goods via the dockyards, their new base would be close by. But there were plenty of places to hide out in a city as old and as tangled as Agatos, particularly down here.

The dockyards were surrounded by a wall with iron spikes embedded in the top, but that was more for show than anything. No self-respecting Warrens thug would let a wall and spikes deter them. A warehouse backed onto the cliffs at the rear. Storage, I assumed, for whatever supplies were needed to repair the ships – wood, tools, ropes ... stuff. A small guard post stood near the front entrance of the warehouse, along with a second by the gates. I settled myself into the shadows of a narrow alley and surveyed the area. Somehow, I was supposed to help the smugglers unload something from a ship, then get it past those guards and into the city without anyone noticing. The guards might be bribed, but a thousand eyes could be watching from the shadows, just like I was now. I would need a big distraction.

A single ship hung from a cradle in a dry dock. The planks had been removed from most of one side and were in the process of being replaced. It wouldn't be going anywhere any time soon. A second, empty dry dock lay beyond it. The smugglers wouldn't want the attention that bringing a ship into the dry dock would attract. Another half dozen ships were tied up alongside small wharfs in front of the dockyards. That would be where they would come in.

Then where? They would have to carry their cargo through the gates, then along the streets, or use a smaller boat to reach another mooring. Either way, they wouldn't want to travel far. Their base would be near the waterfront, too, I reckoned, even if they didn't use a boat. Smugglers would feel most comfortable close to the water, the fucking lunatics. A tavern, a store, or even a warehouse that looked out over the docks. Maybe, like their last hideout, one that had a hidden way to reach the water through a tunnel or sewer.

From here, I could see the dockyards, but I could also see down one of the many steeply sloping alleys that led to the quay. It was busy there. Plenty of dockworkers and sailors moving from bar to brothel to seedy boarding house, but all with their heads down, careful not to meet anyone's eyes. The Watch didn't come this way often, and when they did, they moved through fast, trying to avoid trouble. The smugglers would feel safe around here.

My black mage's cloak was too thick and sweaty for this time of year, but it let me sink into the shadows of the alley, and it was armour against anyone who might come through here looking for an easy mark. Taking on a mage was a fool's game at the best of times, and in this part of town, any mage was likely to be working for the Wren. Interfering with one of his mages was the kind of mistake you only made once.

When I had walked out of my mother's palace five years ago, I hadn't known much about what life as an unaligned mage would involve. I had imagined a busy life of building wards and carrying out jobs that magic would render simple. In reality, it turned out to mainly involve waiting around, and while I usually preferred to do it sitting in a coffee house or bar, more often than not I would find myself propped against an alley wall, waiting for someone to appear. This job, it seemed, wasn't going to be much different, except that I wasn't getting paid. It could be hours before I spotted a smuggler I recognised and was able to trail them to their new base. I was just settling in for a long, uncomfortable night when a stone came out of the shadows of the alley and caught me full on the back of the head.

It didn't knock me out, but it did hurt. I spun around, pulling in magic and raising my mage's rod, to see a bunch of kids fleeing laughing down the alley.

The little shits.

I remembered doing that with Benny when we had been seven or eight, but only to people who didn't belong in the Warrens. We would never have dared to do it to one of our own. Kids were getting bolder.

Or maybe you're not Warrens anymore.

It had been over a decade since I had last lived here. I kept telling myself I was a Warrens kid, but was I? I wasn't Middle City or Grey City. Maybe I wasn't anything, an unanchored boat floating through the shit of the city.

I turned back.

Another stone hit me on the shoulder. I spun again. *Not this time, you bastards.* I threw a magical net.

Mr. Inles's dog had dodged these nets all afternoon, but the stone-thrower wasn't so agile. My net closed about him and tightened, dragging him to the ground. I strode over and stared down at him. He didn't look frightened, just furious as he struggled.

He wasn't getting out of that.

The kid was about seven years old and scrawny, with a narrow face. He reminded me of Benny. Maybe a distant relation. Benny's parents had all but abandoned him when he was only a few years older than this. They could easily have had more children and grandchildren, and we would never have known. Or this could be a cousin's kid. Or someone entirely unrelated. The Warrens bred scrawny, weaselly kids. I considered trying to figure it out, but I doubted Benny would want to know, and I was sure he wouldn't want to know from me.

The other kids had fled. Not much loyalty there. Benny and I wouldn't have fled. We had been painfully loyal to each other, and we had both taken a few beatings for that.

Look at you now. Benny wasn't even talking to me. *Your fault.*

"What do you want?" the kid demanded. "We were only having fun." Still not scared, even trapped with a mage looming over him.

"I need something from you."

"You ain't touching me. I don't do that. I'll fucking knife you."

"I just need information. There's a Mycedan smuggling gang down on the docks, not far from here. Know them?"

"Maybe."

I pulled a silver watchman from my pocket. "Show me, and this is yours."

"Two."

Of course. I released the net, half expecting him to run, but the prospect of the coins seemed to have him entranced.

"Keep up," he said, then darted past me, beckoning me to follow. I did, keeping my magic ready.

We twisted our way through a couple of tight alleys before emerging onto the docks under the shelter of a crumbling tenement.

"There." The boy pointed along the dock-front to where a tavern spilled light onto the cobbles. "That's where they are. Now give me the money."

I eyed him. There was a decent chance the little sod was lying. But this would be an ideal spot for the smugglers. There were enough ships around for this part of the docks to be busy with crews, but far enough from the good part of the city to be safe from regular Watch patrols.

"If you're lying to me," I said, "I can find you, and I'll pull your guts out through your nose." I made magic flare around my hand. It was all show, and I wasn't going to hurt a kid, even if he had been throwing stones at me, but he didn't need to know that.

I gave him a few moments to change his mind, then tossed him the coins. He was gone before his fist had finished closing around them.

I turned my attention to the tavern.

I wasn't going to go barging in there. I had learned my lesson last time, and I didn't want them to know I had found their hideout.

I withdrew to slouch behind a pile of crates with a good view of the entrance and waited again.

CHAPTER FOUR

There was a fair flow of patrons into and out of the tavern, heading to or from ships or stumbling along the docks in search of other places to drink. A couple of them would probably end up in the harbour by the end of the night or knifed in an alley. It was an unusual day when the harbour guard didn't pull a body or two from the water. I even saw a couple I reckoned might be smugglers, but I wasn't sure, and I didn't want to blow my cover.

It was well past midnight, and my legs were starting to throb painfully, despite my mage-boosted stamina, when the door opened again and the leader of the smuggling gang emerged. She gave the docks a quick scan, before heading up a nearby alley.

Thanks, kid.

I let her get a way ahead, then spread a net of magic around me, like seaweed drifting in the waves. I couldn't make myself invisible. I didn't even have enough power to turn eyes away from me. But this would tell me if anyone was watching or following.

I took off after her.

The smuggler was cautious. She paused at intersections, glancing back, around corners, and even above her. But I was able to attach a thread of magic to her and follow from out of sight. I wouldn't be able to track her through the streets if she got too far ahead, but I could make sure she didn't lose me, even when I couldn't actually see her most of the time.

Her route took her deep into the winding streets and alleys of the Warrens. She looked like she knew where she was going, unlike me. A bite of resentment made my teeth clench. This was my place, not hers.

So why have you been avoiding it?

She kept doubling back and taking sudden turns as she navigated her way through the closed-in, twisting streets, but not in the confused way of someone who was lost. With intent. Trying to shake anyone who might be following. And it might have worked, too, if it hadn't been for my thread of magic attached to her. I kept my distance and let the magic lead me.

If you weren't a local, walking in the Warrens was a bad idea, and she wasn't. But the knife at her belt and her demeanour gave her the same protection that my black cloak gave me, stone-throwing kids notwithstanding.

The smuggler reached a more open area, where a couple of small houses had collapsed and no one had cleared away the rubble yet. I hung back and watched her cross the space and disappear into the alley opposite. The thread of magic told me she had stopped just out of sight. Clever. Without the magic, I would have walked out and been seen. I wondered if she was always this paranoid. She wasn't carrying anything smuggled at the moment – she wasn't carrying anything at all, other than her knife – so what was she up to that required such elaborate measures?

Whatever it was, she wasn't catching me out so easily. I could wait here as long as I needed.

A twitch on my net of magic gave me a split second's warning before a voice spoke right behind me. "Well, well, well," the voice said. "Mennik Thorn."

I started, banging my head on the wall I had been pressed against.

For a moment, I thought I had been tailed just as I had been tailing the smugglers' leader. But the woman standing behind me in the alley, fists pressed onto her hips, didn't look like a smuggler. Her long dress was faded, and it wasn't an outfit that would work well on a ship or carrying smuggled goods through a sewer. She was shorter than me by quite a lot – most people were – and her dark hair showed streaks of grey. She seemed to have stepped out of a half-open doorway. Her face did seem familiar, but I couldn't place her.

I glanced over my shoulder, across the open space, to where my quarry was waiting, then hustled this woman back a couple of paces. I hoped her voice hadn't carried. The Warrens were never quiet, even at night, and with luck, her words would have disappeared into the background noise.

"Never thought I'd see you back here." I must have frowned, because she went on, "You don't recognise it, do you?" Now she mentioned it, there was something about the area that resonated, but things changed so abruptly in the Warrens I couldn't pin it down. "That, there." She jabbed a finger at the pile of rubble. "That was your house. Mine was just down here. Still is."

Suddenly, it all clicked into place. This alley we had run up and down so often. There were some new buildings opposite where my house had been, and a passageway that I was sure hadn't been there before, but I could see it, see Benny and me and the other kids fighting and chasing and playing around here. It seemed smaller.

The sight of the one-room home Mica and I had grown up in lying in ruins was like a fist to my stomach. It shouldn't have been. I had hated it here. No, I hadn't hated it. That was wrong. I had hated the way we had to live, the crushing, hungry desperation that insinuated itself into everything here. The miserable confinement, the seeping cold of winter, the inescapable heat of summer, the water and sewage that flowed through the streets when it rained. Despite all of that, the Warrens had been my playground, the limits and the shape of my world. They had defined me and Benny and the other kids as tightly as any dictionary. There had been a kind of pride here. This was our place. We survived it, we made it ours, and no one else helped. The rest of Agatos might as well have been on the other side of the Yttradian Sea. But I had wanted to get out. That home, those limits, the closeness of the walls. I had wanted to be free. I had never understood why my mother stayed here when her powers, influence, and wealth grew. I hadn't known her plans, then. I hadn't known she was just waiting for her time to become the Countess. So, I had resented this place, this cramped home, at the same time that it had delineated me. Now it was nothing. It was gone. It felt like part of me was, too.

"You don't remember me, either, do you? Nik Thorn. You were always too good for the rest of us."

That wasn't fair. I had never thought I was better than the other kids in the Warrens. That had been the way my mother had thought.

"Alena?" I said. I did recognise her, but it had been a long time. She had been about the same age as me and Benny, and we had played in the streets together a long time ago. She looked older, though. The Warrens drained people. "Alena Sand."

"He does remember. Lady of the Grove, a miracle."

A tug on the thread of magic told me the smugglers' leader had moved off again. I couldn't let her get too far ahead or the thread would break. It was taking a lot of effort to keep it connected already.

"Look, I have to go. I'll ... ah ... I'll come back some time. Find you."

"No you won't."

I couldn't stay any longer. I turned and hurried in pursuit.

Eventually, the trail led out of the Warrens on its northern edge, not far from the protruding wedge of Giuffria's Spear. This part of the Middle City might have been better than the Warrens and Dockside, but it certainly wasn't posh. The houses and apartments were larger, the streets wider and planned out. There were even some small gardens and trees, and a couple of public plazas. The looming mass of Giuffria's Spear on one side and the Warrens on the other kept the richest citizens of Agatos away from the neighbourhood. In different circumstances, in a different life, I could have been happy living here.

Most of the inns and coffee houses along the street the smuggler emerged into were still open. With the midsummer days being so hot, most trade happened during the night. I dropped further back and followed.

It didn't take long for the smuggler to choose a busy taverna and duck inside, ignoring the tables in the courtyard out front. I considered following her in, but I wasn't the most inconspicuous person in the city, and I didn't want to blow this now. My sore feet would never forgive me.

I kept the magical thread attached long enough to be sure she was staying put, then let it drop with an exhalation of relief. Maintaining a spell for that long was exhausting.

There had to be a reason why a smuggler would stray this far from Dockside, by such a circuitous route, and it wasn't just for a quiet drink. She didn't want anyone to know she was here.

I stepped back into an alley opposite and resumed waiting.

After half an hour – long enough for the smuggler to have downed a pint or a good-sized glass of wine in her comfortable taverna, while I stood and sweated in a dirty alley – a black-cloaked figure appeared at the end of the street and made her way towards the taverna. Another mage. I unfocused my eyes and confirmed my suspicion. She was using a variation of the spell I had used to see if I was being watched. Now that I could see the dark green magic reaching out from her, it was easy enough to divert any of the strands that drifted too close. I wasn't a powerful mage, but I had always been good at subtlety and fine control, and she didn't even notice me doing it.

Her presence could just be coincidence. This might just be a really great taverna that everyone wanted to visit. Surreptitiously. Making sure they weren't being followed. A kind of anti-Dumonoc's.

I gave it a couple of minutes, then crossed to the taverna. A couple of windows faced the courtyard and the street, thrown open for the cooler night air. I squeezed my way past the packed tables, ignoring the grumbles and protests, until I could peer through the windows. I kept to the side, squinting against the bright light from within.

Through the second window, I saw them. The smuggler sitting with her back to me, the mage opposite, hood pushed partially back, leaning forward and talking earnestly. I couldn't tell what she was saying, but I recognised her. She was one of my mother's mages. I had seen her around the Countess's palace, although I didn't think she had ever talked to me.

What did my mother want with smugglers? The Wren, I could understand. Crime was his thing, and the smugglers were already paying for his protection. But my mother's area of interest was politics. Maybe it was another of her schemes to get one over on her rival. I wondered if she knew the smugglers were threatening my life. I wondered if she cared.

Honestly, I was surprised to see one of my mother's mages at all. My mother, my sister, and most of the other rich and powerful citizens of Agatos had retreated to the cool foothills of Carn's Break, where they would remain for the next couple of months. This mage must have drawn the short straw and been left to look after the Countess's interests in the city. So maybe she wasn't working for my mother after all. Maybe she was taking the opportunity for a side-hustle. I had once believed my mother's mages were fanatically loyal, and some of them were, but the mage Enne Lowriver, who had summoned the ghost of a dead god and framed me for murder, proved that some of them were just pretending. Maybe this mage saw the chance to grab an advantage.

I retreated back to the alley.

I only had to wait another ten minutes before the mage emerged and disappeared back up the street. So. They hadn't just been meeting for a covert shag. Unless it had been a really quick one.

Not long after, the smugglers' leader left the taverna, too. To my surprise, she didn't head back to the docks, but followed the disappearing mage up the street, before taking a quick turn to the left.

What the fuck are you up to?

I guessed I wasn't getting any sleep anytime soon.

The smuggler didn't go far. She found another bar and disappeared inside.

I hoped this wasn't going to go on all night.

This time I had a longer wait – long enough that I had to retreat further into an alley for a quick piss. But eventually, another mage appeared and scurried into the bar, glancing around. He didn't see me; most people were oblivious to things around them, unless they knew what they were doing. If you didn't move or draw attention to yourself, their eyes just slipped past.

I didn't recognise this second mage. He could have been one of my mother's newer minions, an acolyte of the Wren, or one of the late Carnelian Silkstar's mages who hadn't yet attached himself to another high mage. He might even have been a mage directly contracted to one of the richer families, businesses, or the Senate. There weren't many of them, but I never came into contact with them, and I wouldn't know them.

What in the Depths do you all want with a smuggler?

What could she offer them? Whatever it was, I doubted it was good news. Mages' records on fucking things up for everyone else were second to none.

This is what the smugglers are dragging you into. It wasn't a comforting thought.

~

Even Agatos was beginning to close down for the night by the time I finally got back to my apartment. I had been up too long again, and I was ready to collapse.

Unfortunately, a now-familiar figure was once again sitting on my front steps.

Dumonoc.

I spun on my heel and had taken a couple of good strides away before I heard him call out, "Thorn! I want to talk to you."

Fuck.

Slowly, I turned and trudged back. "What do you want, Dumonoc? It's late." Not that I would have been any happier to see him earlier.

"You didn't do your job."

Last time I had seen Dumonoc, he had called me a bastard and banned me from his shitty bar. It didn't exactly make me feel warm and friendly towards him. "What the fuck are you talking about?"

"You didn't break the curse."

Nope. No. This was too much. "Yeah. I did. Your drinks were cursed. I broke the curse. It was gone."

I had checked thoroughly. The curse had collapsed, and there had been no trace of it left. I would have seen it. I might not be powerful, but I wasn't incompetent. Anyway, a broken curse always collapsed. It didn't hang around.

"And now it's back." Dumonoc wasn't as tall as me, but

he could match me in belligerence, and he was standing a couple of steps above me.

I came closer until we were almost nose-to-nose. "That's not how curses work. When they're gone, they're gone. Unless you've got yourself cursed again. Maybe you pissed off the wrong person." Mages could be petty. I should know.

"Fix it."

"And how am I supposed to do that if I'm never allowed back in your bar?"

For a moment I thought he was going to headbutt me, and I'd already started dropping my chin so he would catch the top of my head instead of my face. Instead, his teeth ground together like rocks on the beach in a storm. "I'll pay you. Again."

I smiled. "Now that's what I like to hear." I held out a hand. "Same fee."

Honestly, if I had thought of it before, I might have cursed the place myself as a nice little earner.

I waited until he had counted out the silver watchmen with the reluctance and speed of a man pulling out his own fingernails.

"Good," I said. "Now piss off and let me get some sleep. I'll be there tomorrow morning."

CHAPTER FIVE

THE NEXT MORNING DAWNED EVEN HOTTER THAN THE LAST, and I had come in too tired and too late to fetch water from the public pipe half a block up. I was thirsty, I stank of sweat, and I had nowhere to wash. If I had been going anywhere else other than Dumonoc's, I might have cared.

My route took me through the eastern side of the Middle City, then across the Royal Highway to the Grey City. There hadn't been a royal in Agatos since the Godkiller, Agate Blackspear, had died, but the man had loved naming things after himself, starting with the city itself and certainly not ending with the Royal Highway. Even four hundred years later, no one had quite got up the courage to rename things. Blackspear had been a high mage, after all, and had killed the patron goddess of the city in a duel. A few centuries of death were not enough for most people to be certain he wouldn't take offence. Above all else, the citizens of Agatos were a practical people.

A small, excited crowd had gathered outside a temple to the old Melaruan war god, Ethys. I caught fragments of conversation from the crowd. Miracles. Signs. All the usual bollocks. I had a very simple relationship with religion: I would keep well away from it, and it could keep well away from me. Even so, I was tempted to sneak a look at whatever trickery the priests were up to to bleed money from their followers. But I resisted.

See? I had learned some lessons.

Ethys was a dead god and had been dead since the Melaruan empire had decided that there was more money to be made in trade than in sticking spears into their neighbours and getting spears back in return. I didn't know if the two events were linked. Maybe someone had stuck a spear in Ethys.

In a trade city like Agatos, people brought their religion with them, even if their gods were long gone and about as much use as an iron chain to a drowning man. In my experience, temples to dead gods were larger, grander, and more tasteless than temples to living gods, the hope being, I assumed, that if the worshippers just tried hard enough, their god might stop being dead and answer some damned prayers. It didn't work that way. I had seen the ghost of a dead god, and I had seen a forgotten god rise, but dead gods didn't come back. Dead was dead. Anyway, it wasn't like the living gods bothered answering prayers either. The temple to Ethys was no exception to the rule. It loomed over the neighbouring buildings. I gave the whole thing a wide berth.

Dumonoc's was closed this early in the day, but I hammered happily on the door until he finally opened it, looking disgusted.

"Right, then," I said, rubbing my hands together and smiling. Dumonoc's foul temper always cheered me up. "Let's see the drinks."

Dumonoc stepped aside and let me in. "It's not the drink this time. It's the food."

"You serve food? How come I never knew?"

"You never asked."

Well, with the drinks he offered, it had never crossed my mind. I didn't have a death wish. "Where is it?"

Dumonoc walked around the bar, then opened the door at the back. I followed him. The kitchen beyond was surprisingly well lit and clean after the gloomy bar. Sinks had been scrubbed to a gleam, immaculate pans hung from hooks, neatly ordered spices were arranged on shelves, and fresh herbs in bunches lay on the counter.

"This is what you cook?" I should have asked about food a long time ago. How come I had never seen him serve any? Maybe he was right that I really had scared away all his best customers.

"Fuck, no. You bastards wouldn't appreciate it. This is for my family."

"You have kids?" It had been enough of a shock to find out he was married, but the idea of the miserable old sod having children just hurt my brain.

"A sister. Nephews and nieces. And none of them are any of your fucking business. Sort out your mess." He jabbed a finger towards a counter on the far side of the kitchen, near a second door.

I didn't have to get too close to see there was something wrong. The smell of rot was enough to tell me. Vegetables had browned and were liquifying, collapsing in on themselves even as I watched. Mould grew like hair on blocks of cheese. Maggots squirmed on meat. The stink and the sight almost made me throw up.

"When did this start?"

"Yesterday afternoon. It kept spreading, and I kept putting it back here while I waited for you to finally turn up."

So, it hadn't begun until after I had dealt with the curse on the drinks out front.

"If you had shown me back here yesterday, we might not have this problem." I didn't think that was true, but if Dumonoc wanted to try to blame me for this mess, I would be more than happy to shift it back onto him.

I unfocused my eyes and once again saw the almost-living sea-blue net of magic slipping organically over the food, while tendrils reached across the kitchen towards the herbs and spices.

The wrongness of it hit me again. Curses didn't behave this way. Not unless some very clever mage had come up with an entirely new type of curse just to spite Dumonoc. Which would have been fully justified in my opinion, although unlikely.

But it was still a curse, and I knew what to do with it. It took me only a minute to collapse it and let the magic drain away, then another five to scan the whole damned place, kitchen and bar, to make sure there really were no traces remaining.

It was gone. I was absolutely sure this time.

"Most likely thing is that someone came back and cursed you again after I got rid of the first one," I said. "You must have enemies." He absolutely must. Not everyone was as sanguine about being insulted on a regular basis. "Who dislikes you enough to want to trash your business?"

"You."

"Funny." But he had a point. The list of people who hated him might stretch half way around Agatos and include anyone who had ever found themselves in this miserable hole. I would have to try a different angle. "Right. Then tell me everyone who was in here both days before the curses took hold."

He thought for a moment, then grabbed a piece of paper and scribbled for a few seconds, before handing it to me. I peered at it.

"That's all? You're sure?"

"Yeah."

"All right." There were three names listed. Well, two names and one really unhelpful description. "Tall Agatos man, short hair, brown shirt with tear in back. That's it? You didn't ask his name?"

"What the fuck do you think this place is? I only knew

your name because you insisted in fucking introducing yourself like I gave a toss."

Lovely. "And did you tell this man to fuck off?"

"Maybe."

"Hmm." Wandering into a bar and being told to fuck off would certainly be enough to anger a lot of people. But I wasn't going to find him based on that description. "Do you know what time he came in?"

"Midday. Reckon he must have finished an early shift. Probably at the docks."

"Both times?"

He nodded. Well, midday was still a way off. Maybe the guy would come back, and I could see if he was my man. In the meantime, I had the other two.

"We can write off Squint," I said. I had spent enough time in the same bar as Squint to know he didn't even have any latent magical potential. Which just left me with one name. "Bardon Hail. Severan Street. You don't know where exactly?"

Dumonoc's expression of contempt was enough to answer that one.

"Fine. I'll find out if he's behind this, but only because this is an interesting case. I'm not doing it for you."

Dumonoc smiled for the first time since I had known him. "In that case, I ain't paying."

Severan Street wasn't the kind of place you would expect to find a mage, even an angry one. Which was ironic, bearing in mind that it was exactly where I was.

All right. Any angry mage except me. And I wasn't living down here. Money came easily to most mages – again, except me. There were always people willing to pay for what magic could do. If it hadn't been for my stupid principles – and my damage, I had to admit – I could have been wealthy. If there was a mage down here, he would have to be even more fucked up than I was.

The narrow street ran down from the Grey City into the edge of Fishertown. The houses on either side were small, close, and in poor repair. When the Grey City had been built – back before it became the Grey City – it had been for the newly-wealthy of Agatos, grown rich on trade. Open plazas, spacious houses, public forums, parks... But even back then, no one had wanted to live too close to Fishertown with its all-pervading smell of fish.

Fishertown had once been a village of its own on the eastern bank of the Erastes river, hard against the harbour, a cluster of tight fishermen's houses and yards. It had never truly become a part of Agatos. My stepfather – Mica's dad – had been from Fishertown. So was Mica's boyfriend ... partner ... whatever the fuck I was supposed to call him. But mixing between Fishertown and the rest of the city was rare, and the way this street closed in as it approached Fishertown ensured that no one would casually wander in.

Of course, as the wealthy had become more wealthy – money flowed to the already rich as immutably as water flowed down to the sea – they had abandoned the Grey City and made for the even more refined and elevated Upper City, leaving the Grey City to crumble. Severan Street seemed to have taken more than its fair share of crumbling.

Dumonoc hadn't been able to provide me with an exact address for Bardon Hail, so I took the easiest option. I hammered on the first door I came to until it was answered.

A woman of about my age eyed me suspiciously from behind the half-open door. I heard kids shouting from inside. She looked tired and harried. Her eyes went to my black cloak, and they tightened with fear.

This fucking cloak. I should never have worn it. It was already making me sweat, and it scared people. What did that say about the mages of Agatos that just the sight of a black cloak brought fear? If I had been the Ash Guard, I would have come down harder on the bastards.

Like you don't use it for your own ends whenever you can.

I wondered what I was even doing down here. This wasn't my business. Dumonoc had made it clear that he wouldn't pay me. He hadn't asked me to do this. And what did I care if he wanted to keep getting himself cursed? I didn't owe him anything. Benny would have told me how stupid I was being. If he had been here. If he had been talking to me. He would have told me to keep my nose out of other people's problems, only he wouldn't have said it so politely.

I raised my hands placatingly, but it only made the woman flinch.

"I'm just looking for someone. Bardon Hail. Do you know where he lives?"

She shook her head, then retreated, closing the door firmly in my face.

Right.

I knew mages weren't popular, particularly in the lower city. Depths, mages weren't popular with *me*. But this reaction was extreme. A mage must have been down here throwing their power about. This Hail, maybe?

It took me another three houses and a lot of nervous people before a man pointed to a house with flaking plaster and windows shuttered with rotting wood.

I pulled in raw magic as I approached and readied my shield spell. If Hail had been behind the curse, he was no amateur, and I doubted he would be pleased to see me.

This door took a whole load more thumping than the previous ones before a male voice finally answered and cordially invited me to fuck off. I decided to take that as an invitation.

I popped the lock and went in with my shield up, a spear of magic ready to throw.

A muffled voice of protest came from behind one of the doors on the far side of the cluttered room. I picked my way through the junk and dirt and kicked it open.

The bedroom beyond boasted two tattered mattresses, a ragged curtain across a broken, shuttered window, and a small pile of discarded clothes between the mattresses.

Only one of the mattresses was occupied. A half-dressed man sat up from under a filthy blanket, shielding bloodshot eyes with one hand.

"What the fuck?" he managed.

"Bardon Hail?"

He grabbed for a knife lying beside his mattress. I sent a bolt of magic into it, and it fizzed. He snatched his hand back.

"I'll take that as a yes?"

The room stank. I didn't smell too good myself, but this was something else. Hail was sweating old beer, and at some point he had thrown up and not cleaned it away. I could see it dried on his chin.

Pity!

"You've been in Dumonoc's the last couple of days."

"I didn't steal anything!"

He had definitely stolen something. "What were you doing there?"

He looked at me like I was an idiot. "I can't afford anywhere else anymore, can I?"

"Anymore?"

He turned his head and spat. It dribbled down his chin onto the dried puke. It made me want to throw up, too.

"Not after those bastards."

Bastards? He was resentful about someone. That was promising.

"Which bastards?"

"Which bastards? Who the fuck do you think? I used to have a good job. Down in the warehouses. Wool, you know? Stacking and sorting and carrying. Good work.

Then some bastard took it over and brought in their own people and that was it. Bastards."

So, he had lost his job. That didn't seem like a reason to be pissed off with Dumonoc.

"This your place?"

Hail looked around, as though seeing it for the first time. "Just staying here for a while. Until I get things together again."

By the looks of it, that wasn't happening any time soon.

I unfocused my eyes to look for traces of magic, anything that might suggest this man or whoever else lived here was a mage. There was a small trickle of raw magic flowing into Hail, but that didn't make him a mage. A lot of people had a trace of natural magical ability, and while this might be enough to make any curse he threw marginally effective, there was no way he could have cast the one on Dumonoc's food and drink. That would take real, controlled power. His pathetic trickle of magic might be the only thing keeping him alive at the moment, but it certainly hadn't caused Dumonoc's problems. I doubted he even knew he was doing it.

This had been a bust. Another name off Dumonoc's list. Which just left the man who had turned up at around midday the last couple of days and about whom Dumonoc had been able to tell me absolutely nothing useful at all.

CHAPTER SIX

MAGES – EVEN UNTRAINED, NATURAL MAGES – COULD sustain ourselves longer than other people without food or drink, as my new friend on the mattress had proven. We healed quicker, and we could keep going longer. Our bodies used raw magic to maintain themselves. But even the most powerful mages had to eat and drink eventually, and I was not the most powerful mage. In fact, I was starving.

I had got into the habit of eating at a small place only a street from my apartment. It wasn't a fully-fledged taverna, just a single room with a few tables and chairs and a couple of counters. The food was simple but cheap, it did the job, and nobody bothered me. And, unlike when I prepared my own food, I'd never ended up with food poisoning here.

I settled myself in for a midmorning meal and let myself think everything through. All this shit with

Dumonoc, all this chasing around after whoever might have cursed his shitty drinks, that was me avoiding my real problem. But it wasn't a problem I could avoid for much longer. In two and half days, the smugglers would be bringing in some unknown cargo, and I would have to be there to hide it from spying eyes. *Then they'll have you. You'll be theirs for as long as they want you.*

Chances were, those meetings the smugglers' leader had gone to last night were about the cargo. Why else would she need a mage to keep it hidden? The smugglers had lost their own mage weeks ago. They must have brought in cargo during that time, but they hadn't come to me.

It has to be something magical. You know it does.

Like this city needed more magical shit fucking everything up.

Mages had different ambitions. Wealth, power, influence, acclaim. But at the root of it, the tool that only mages could use to reach those desires, was magic.

Nothing to do with mages was ever good. *And here you are, helping some mage achieve their fucked up ambition.*

I was running out of time to figure a way out of all this. On the other hand, it wasn't far off midday. Dumonoc's final suspect would be reaching the bar soon, if he followed his recent pattern. I would have a chance to intercept him. Maybe I could discover exactly how he had managed that curse, before I kicked his arse and told him never to come back.

For fuck's sake! I thumped my table, making the server

behind the counter look up with a frown. I raised a hand in apology. I had to stop procrastinating. I had to stop putting off my problems until it was too late. All it did was cause me far more shit. Dumonoc's curse was hardly the most pressing matter. *Find out what the smugglers are doing. Stop them, if it comes to that. Then worry about Dumonoc.*

For once, I was going to learn my lesson. For once, I was going to make the right choice.

THE DOCKS WERE BLINDING AT THIS TIME OF DAY. SUNLIGHT glittered as sharp as glass from the water and reflected back from the whitewashed walls. Even the work of loading and unloading ships and bringing in catches had paused in the face of the unrelenting heat. There was a strange, heavy stillness to the place. There wasn't even a breeze off the water. Other than a few guards on the ships or beside warehouses – and one second-rate mage who should have known better – the only signs of life were a few seagulls floating high overhead, occasionally calling to one another, and couple of sprawled dogs in the shade of a building. Even the smugglers' new tavern looked dead, with shutters and door firmly closed against the heat of the day.

I pushed inside. The air within was stuffy and hot, an oppressive presence thick with the smell of old beer and sweat. Only a dozen people occupied the tavern bar, and most of them seemed half asleep. But the woman I was looking for was among them. The leader of the smugglers was sitting in the shadows at the back of the room, eyes fixed on me as I strode over.

I pulled out a chair and sat opposite her. "We need to talk."

"You're not very bright, are you, mage?"

I glanced over my shoulder. The sleepy patrons of the tavern seemed to have perked up, and half a dozen firearms were now aimed my way. The skin on my back crawled. Maybe this hadn't been such a great idea after all. *So much for learning your lesson.* I forced myself to turn back to my target. I didn't think her minions would be stupid enough to open fire with their boss sitting so close, but I put up shield anyway. *Better hope it catches all the bullets.* It wasn't something I had ever put to the test.

"You want me to help you bring something into the city," I said, keeping my voice level, despite my racing pulse.

"It is not a negotiation. You *will* bring it in."

"I have no problem with that." I did have a problem with that. "But if I'm going to do it effectively, I need to know more. What are you bringing in? Where are you taking it?"

Her lips spread into a grin. "I'm sure you know I won't tell you that."

It had been worth a try, but no, I hadn't been expecting it. "It makes a difference. If I have to hide something the size of a ship, I'll have to prepare differently than if it's the size of my fist."

She rubbed at the blue tattoo beside her eye. Then she seemed to make a decision. "It's a box. A small chest." She held her hands twice her shoulder-width apart. "About that big. You will have to hide it for no more than half an hour. We have a place prepared for it."

Prepared. Interesting word. What kind of preparation would you need for a box? Now if there was something magical inside that box...

"You will get it there," she continued. "And, no, I will not tell you where that is."

Yeah, and when I got it there, what was she was planning to do to stop me telling anyone about it? A knife in the back? A rain of bullets? If she thought I was walking into that, she was the one who wasn't very bright.

I stood. "Fine. I can work with that." I hoped I wouldn't have to. If I got to that stage, I would be in big trouble.

"Mr. Thorn. You should know that I am not pleased you have discovered where we work once more. It disturbs me. It was unwise of you."

I met her eyes, unflinching despite the pounding of blood in my ears. "Yeah, well. Life's full of disappointments."

I kept my expression flat as I nodded towards the armed smugglers still pointing their guns at me, then walked steadily out the door. I made it all the way to the nearest alley before I had to drop to my haunches and finally let the shivers run through me.

That had been a pretty stupid move. *How did you think it was going to turn out?* If they had ever intended to let me walk free after the job, they would now be rethinking that plan. But I had my answer, and I knew what I had to do. I just didn't know how to manage it.

~

THE WAY I SAW IT, I HAD THREE OPTIONS: HIDE, FIGHT, OR get someone else to do the fighting for me.

Hide, I could do, but not in Agatos. Agatos was an honest city. Not honest as in, wouldn't lie, cheat, steal, or murder. But honest as in, if someone wanted something enough, someone else would sell it to them. That was doubly true when it came to information. I would be found eventually.

But Agatos wasn't the whole world. I could join a caravan to the northern cities, Khorasan, Rannoni, even all the way up to Lidhara. The smugglers would have no influence up there. Or I could take a ship, sail to Tor or Secellia. I had always thought my father must have come from one of those countries on the western edge of the Yttradian Sea. One day, I had always told myself, I would go there and find out. I had never left Agatos at all. Now would be the perfect time. But the thought of being chased out by these bastards, of never being able to return, sent a surge of visceral revulsion through me. This was *my* city. Not theirs.

So maybe I could fight. One-on-one, with my magic to back me up, I could take them. Depths, I could probably take six or seven of them. But was I really going to spend my days hunting smugglers through the streets and docks of Agatos, hoping to catch them before they caught me?

And then what? Murder them one at a time? That wasn't the kind of person I was, and if I did manage it, that wasn't the kind of person I wanted to become.

That just left one option.

The last time I had gone to Captain Gale for help she had sent me packing. Things had changed since then. Now I knew – well, *thought* ... suspected – the smugglers were bringing in something magical. That made it Ash Guard business, and Captain Gale wouldn't thank me for not sharing this information. At least that was what I told myself. If I believed it hard enough, it had to be true, right?

I left the smugglers' tavern behind and headed back along the docks, carefully trailing my magic behind me as I went. It was a good precaution, because shortly after I left, someone followed me out and along the docks.

I had been expecting a tail. They needed me, but they didn't trust me any more than I trusted them. Heading directly for the Ash Guard was out. Instead, I went home. Let them think I was retreating from the heat of the afternoon like a rational person.

I waited until the smuggler took up position in the shade of a doorway twenty yards down the street, then let myself in and headed past my narrow office into the warded section of my apartment.

It was hot and stuffy here, too. I could have expended magical energy keeping it cool, but it would have drained me, and it was still a relief after the sun-beaten streets.

I dumped my stupid woollen black cloak, changed to a cleaner, dry shirt, and pulled on a light, blue jacket that I had bought in the Penitent's Ear a couple of weeks ago. It was really too warm for this time of year, which was why it had been cheap, but it did serve as a superficial disguise, especially when combined with a low, floppy hat. I might look like an arsehole, but at least I didn't look like a mage.

Then, I opened a back window, checked with my magic that the smuggler was still at his post, and scrambled out and down into the tiny yard and footway that backed onto these houses. It was this easy escape route that had helped persuade me to rent this place.

Even so, I didn't head directly for the Ash Guard fortress. I followed last night's example of the smugglers' leader and chose an indirect, circuitous route, taking me through the lower parts of the Middle City and the Warrens.

By the time I reached the Ash Guard fortress, I was certain I hadn't been followed, but I still took a minute at the edge of the plaza to check if anyone was watching. The lazy heat radiated from the paving in shimmers of distorted air. From somewhere nearby, from the rocky, straggly slopes at the bottom of Giuffria's Spear, I could hear the high creaking of grasshoppers.

Now or never. I pushed down my nerves and strode across the plaza, shoulders tense against a shout or a shot that never came.

Captain Gale looked like she had been sleeping when she emerged, but to be fair, she seemed to always be out on patrol or sleeping. As far as I could tell, she had no social life. Not that I was much better. Her face pulled into a one-sided smile when she saw me.

"How did I know it was going to be you?"

"Was it the lovely, warm feeling in the pit of your stomach?"

She snorted. "That was my dinner last night disagreeing with me." She eyed me up and down. "Nice hat, by the way. And, no, I don't mean that."

Time to change the subject before she completely punctured my ego. "You remember that smuggling gang I told you about?"

"It was only yesterday, Nik. I haven't completely lost my mind, despite your best attempts. I also remember telling you it wasn't my province."

"Yeah, well, I wasn't entirely honest with you. They do have a new mage."

Her expression turned serious, hard. I felt a little shiver of terror. Sometimes I forgot she could and would kill me if she thought I was a danger to the city. I didn't even know if she would regret it.

"And this mage? Have they been stepping out of line in my city like the last one?"

How was I supposed to answer that? "He wouldn't dream of it."

Her eyes narrowed. "What have you done, Nik?"

Fuck. "Nothing! They're just ... ah ... they're forcing me to help them bring in a cargo."

"Then go to the Watch, for Pity's sake, just like I told you."

I wet my lips. It really was too hot out here. "They're bringing in something magical."

"You're sure?"

Kind of sure. I nodded.

"You never bring good news, do you?"

I bristled. "You asked me to tell you when trouble was coming, remember? Well, trouble *is* coming, and I'm not the one who caused it."

She hadn't even asked me to let her know. She had told me flat out that I had to. I'd got the very real idea that if I didn't, she would blame me for anything that happened. She had already arrested me a couple of times, and I didn't fancy a third.

"What was I thinking?" She sighed. "Come on. I need breakfast."

She took me to the small coffee house not far from the Ash Guard fortress that she had taken me to once before, and while she was eating, I told her everything. Well, not everything. I didn't tell her how I had started the whole feud with the smuggling gang by bursting into their previous headquarters and kicking the shit out of several of them, including their mage. I also made myself sound much snappier and more competent than I actually had been, but from her expression, I didn't think she bought it.

"Whatever it is, they're bringing it in in two days. I'm supposed to meet them on the Dragon's Jaw. They'll have a small boat waiting to take me to the ship. Then we'll sail into the dockyards where I'm supposed to keep whatever it is hidden until they get it to its destination. No more than half an hour, they said."

"Hmm." She paused, tapping her finger on the side of her plate. "All right. You're going to have to go through with it."

My jaw dropped. "What? Come off it. I can't go out there." Mica's dad had died on the waters of the Erastes Bay, his body lost, his boat broken on the waves. He had been a fisherman, an experienced sailor who knew the waters and the weather as well as I knew the city, but it hadn't saved him. Ever since he had drowned, I had experienced a terror of the deep water. And I had come face-to-gaping-maw with some of the things that haunted the depths below, things with cruel teeth, dagger-sharp claws, and wet, black eyes. "Can't you just..." I waved a hand in the vague direction of the harbour. "You know?"

"Board the ship? Out there on the Erastes Bay, just on your say-so? We would need ships, dozens of soldiers. A lot of people could die." She set her knife on her plate, as though I had put her off the whole idea of breakfast. "Depths, how would we even know which was the right ship? There'll be dozens out there, waiting to come to port or to pass through the Bone Straits. You want us to board them all, one after another?" She sat back, shaking her head. "Anyway, have you considered it might be a test?"

"A test?"

"You know. To see if you're betraying them. We go charging in, there's nothing to be found, they know you tipped us off. Oh, yeah. And the whole Ash Guard are pissed off at you for wasting our time and effort."

It made sense. I just didn't want it to.

"Do exactly what they tell you. I'll have a squad waiting near the dockyards. When you have the item, give us a signal and we'll deal with it and them. All you'll have to do is keep out of the way, which I know is not your strong point, but which you will do very carefully this time. If there is nothing, if it's a test, you'll stay quiet, and you'll have passed. When the real cargo comes in, they'll trust you."

"You can't just arrest them now?" I said plaintively.

"We still have to follow the law, Nik. No proof, nothing we can do."

Again, it made sense. But I couldn't help but feel this was going to go horribly wrong. "What kind of signal?"

She grinned. "You'll think of something. Knowing you, it'll be hard to miss." She must have noticed the disconsolate expression on my face, because she added, "Cheer up. I'll even buy you a pastry. After it's all done, of course. We'll call it expenses."

CHAPTER SEVEN

I SAT IN THE COFFEE HOUSE FOR A WHILE AFTER CAPTAIN Gale had gone, hands wrapped around my iced coffee, staring at nothing. I really had imagined Captain Gale and her squad swooping down on the smugglers, giving them a good kicking, and dragging them off to gaol. I had been sure I had found a way out, to free myself from the smugglers once and for all. Instead, I was left hoping they would dock exactly where I expected, Captain Gale and her people would be waiting close enough, and no one would put a bullet in the back of my head in the chaos.

Any plan that relied on everything going according to plan was a plan that was going to go wrong.

I could go back and tell Captain Gale it was off. But then what? I would be back where I started, spending every moment watching over my shoulder for the rest of my no-doubt too-short life.

That was the problem with working with the authorities: they had rules and procedures. I understood why. I wouldn't want it any other way, really. If anything, the city needed to apply the rules more strictly and to everyone, even the wealthy and influential. The Ash Guard were accountable only to themselves – and, I supposed, in extremis to the Senate if they got completely out of hand – but the Ash Guard's own rules were rigid, and I had known Captain Gale long enough to know she wouldn't act without being sure. It was the reason I had survived my first encounter with her.

No, if I wanted to get myself out of this, I was going to have to follow the plan through to the end and hope Captain Gale was good enough to cover all eventualities.

I needed a drink. Depths, it might be one of the last drinks I ever had. I reckoned Dumonoc owed me something from one of those good bottles he claimed he stocked.

I headed down through the Middle City, then turned east on Long Step Avenue until I reached the Royal Highway. The commotion outside the Temple of Ethys had grown since this morning, and the crowd almost blocked the street, despite the punishing heat of the afternoon. A group of sweaty, irritated Watchwomen and -men were working to corral the crowd and keep the main highway clear enough for the carts and caravans, which even now clattered up and down the cobbles.

"None of your business, Nik," I reminded myself. Getting involved with gods never ended well.

I determinedly ignored the fuss and headed into the Grey City, towards Dumonoc's bar.

You might have thought that, having twice saved his business from a curse, Dumonoc would be happier to see me. But you would have been wrong. The look of disgust on his face was enough to warm my heart.

It was cool down here, below ground level, and the bar was relatively busy. I counted a dozen people sitting around their little pools of candlelight.

"Ever thought about giving them a bit more light?" I said as I approached the bar.

"Ever thought of fucking off?"

It was the high quality of Dumonoc's banter that brought me back here. I drew up a stool. "Just trying to help. If your customers didn't have to worry about tripping over and breaking their necks, they might come back more often."

"It's atmospheric."

"You mean it hides the dirt."

His expression turned as sour as his wine. "What the fuck is that on your head?"

I touched my floppy hat. "Do you like it?"

"No. You look like a twat."

Right. Well, no one was coming to Dumonoc for fashion advice. "Give me a drink. From one of those good bottles you told me about."

"I'm not wasting that on you."

How exactly had Dumonoc persuaded some poor sod to marry him? "I thought you might be a bit more grateful, what with me spending all day trying to track down who cursed you." Well, part of the day. A couple of hours in the morning.

"I never asked you to."

"True. But when the curse happens again, and you come to me begging for help, I can always charge you more."

His lips twisted, but he reached under the bar and came up with a bottle. He poured a miserly sample into a cup. "Don't just fucking down it. This is good stuff."

I tried a sip, half expecting it to eat away at my teeth like his normal drinks, but it wasn't bad. Not great, but not bad. I suspected he still wasn't sharing his best stuff with me. I set it down.

"Bardon Hail didn't curse you. I checked him out. He couldn't curse a sparrow, even if he was sober, and I don't think he's often sober."

"Never thought he'd be the one."

I frowned. "Then why did you give me his name?"

Dumonoc shrugged.

Fuck me. "Right, then. This other bloke. Has he been in today?"

"Yeah. He's over there, that table near the door."

I turned and eyed the man. He was an Agatos native, maybe ten or fifteen years older than me, a Grey City resident from the quality of his clothes. Respectable, just, but not in any way wealthy. He had noticed Dumonoc point him out and was watching me with nervous eyes.

"Oi!" I shouted, displaying my usual charm. "I want a word with you."

That didn't have the effect I had hoped for. The man leapt to his feet and bolted. He was through the door before I could push myself off my stool.

"Wait!" I shouted, which had about as much success as it normally did.

Bannaur's balls. I took off in pursuit.

The man was halfway across the small plaza by the time I reached street level. I was pretty fast, but this guy was a sprinter. I was never going to catch him. I pulled in raw magic, shaped it, and sent a burst of force to tangle around his legs. He fell forwards, planting his face on the paving stones.

If he really was a mage, I wouldn't have much time. I raced over, flipped him onto his back, and brought a blade of magic slashing down at this throat. This would be when a mage reacted, throwing up a shield, disrupting my spell, or launching his own attack. I was prepared to block anything he cast. But there was nothing. My magical blade wasn't visible, but any mage would have known it was there. The man wasn't even looking at it. He was just staring up at me while blood streamed from his nose.

"What were you doing in Dumonoc's?" I demanded.

"I just wanted a drink, that's all. Just a drink."

"Goat shit. No one wants Dumonoc's drinks. Why were you really there? What do you have against Dumonoc?"

Stupid question. He had met Dumonoc. That was enough.

"Nothing!" Blood bubbled from his nose. He tried to shake it away. "I just wanted to make a good impression."

"On Dumonoc? He doesn't even know who you are. Why the fuck would you want to make a good impression?"

The man deflated. He lifted an arm to wipe away the blood, and I let him. I had a horrible, growing feeling that I was making a terrible mistake here.

"I just ... I was just going to ask his sister to walk out with me. I thought it would turn out better if he liked me."

Fuck! "Why did you run?"

"I've seen you before. You're a mage..." He let it trail off, but I understood. Mages were arseholes. They abused their power and privilege. No one in their right mind wanted to be noticed by one. I had just shown him exactly why that was.

I climbed off him. "You're wasting your time. Dumonoc doesn't like anyone." I offered him a hand and helped him up. "Um." I gestured to his bloody nose and now-filthy clothes. "Sorry about all this."

I watched him scamper off. What a fuck up. I headed back to Dumonoc's.

"Well?" Dumonoc said as I reached the bar and sat again.

I shook my head. "Not him either."

"Magnificent. So you just chased off another one of my customers. You're fucking ruining me, Thorn."

"Oh, he'll be back." I hoped. Unless I had scared him off for good. "Maybe offer him a free drink."

"Right. Why not just give it all away? Who needs to

make a living?" He raised his voice. "Free drinks for everyone!" Heads popped up at that. "Settle down! What the fuck do you think this is?" He glared at me. "Arsehole."

I unfocused my eyes and took a slow look around the bar. Nothing unusual. "There's no curse here right now. Keep a good eye out for anyone or anything suspicious and fetch me if it happens again."

The look Dumonoc gave me carried every ounce of disgust he could muster. "Oh, just fuck off, Mennik."

My route back home didn't need to take me past the Temple of Ethys. But I'd have to take a detour to avoid it, and Depths, I did have *some* self-control. It wasn't like I was going to get involved. I had enough to worry about. Anyway, I was curious to see how long people would stand out in the sun and heat in the hope of something religious happening.

The answer to that was a fuck of a long time. If anything, the crowd had grown again, and it had attracted the usual constellation of hawkers flogging drinks, food, and hastily modified religious icons. If someone didn't do something about it soon, this would evolve into a full-on religious festival that would still be celebrated two hundred years from now, even if by then everyone had forgotten what had started it.

Still none of your business.

But, fuck it, what the Depths was going on?

"Why do you care?" I muttered.

"Because it could mean trouble," I answered myself. "You don't want to get blindsided."

Which was a goat shit excuse. There was no reason to think whatever was happening there would have anything to do with me ever.

Unless you stick your nose in. I had learned better than that.

"Just a quick look," I muttered. "Just to see."

It would keep eating at me until I knew.

So much for self-control. So much for learning my lesson.

A quick look can't hurt.

That was going to be my epitaph.

I worked my way through the crowd to the temple doors. Here the crush was too tight to push through, and I didn't have my mage's cloak to open the way. The priests at the door were doing their best to manage the flow, guiding worshippers out on one side and slowly letting more in on the other. I could see over the heads around me, but the interior of the temple was too dark after the searing brightness of the street, and I couldn't make out what the excitement was all about. I noticed the priests were holding out bags for donations before letting anyone in. This must have been a profitable day for them. The bags looked heavy.

I waited in the middle of the sweaty crowd until I finally shuffled my way into the temple, free of the heat and several coins lighter.

The Temple of Ethys had stood in Agatos for a couple

of hundred years, the fervour of the god's devotees not at all diminished by their god being dead, and the priests hadn't wasted their time. There was gold everywhere, a garish, glistering display of wealth and lack of imagination. If there was a surface, carving, protrusion, or perfectly innocent piece of furniture, someone had smeared it with gold. What a dead god would want with all of this was beyond me. It must have impressed someone, I supposed. Maybe my donated coins would help add to this overbearing display.

No one seemed to be here for the gold, though. They were all transfixed by the altar, and I could see why. Ten feet above it, an enormous stone statue of a figure wielding a spear and shield and with the face of an eagle rotated slowly in the air. Ethys, I supposed. What he was doing up there, I had no idea.

I turned to one of the nearby priests. "Ah... Does it always do that?"

The priest's eyes were wide with wonder – or maybe she was just trying to fight off exhaustion if she'd been here all day.

"It usually floats." She held her hands a few inches apart. "Not so high, though. Ethys is returning, praise his arms."

"Yeah, all right. Praise his arms."

I moved closer. Dead gods didn't return. That was the point of being dead. But priests, well, I wouldn't put anything past them. It would be an unusual temple that didn't use a combination of magic, hallucinatory drugs, and the gullible fervour of its worshippers to keep them enthusiastic. I unfocused my eyes.

Yep. Just as I suspected. The statue wasn't being held up by the power of a god. It was magic, plain and simple. A spell had been woven into the statue. It looked old, and it must have been cast to keep the statue hovering above the altar. The principle was the same as placing a ward. You needed a magical structure to automatically convert raw magic to keep powering the spell without the casting mage being present. In the case of a ward, the sustained effect could be an alarm, a barrier, or a spell to disintegrate you. The statue's magic was simpler. All it needed was to raise the lump of holy stone and keep it steady.

It was quite possible that most of the priests had no idea their god wasn't responsible for this. But there was a clear difference between the power of a god and magic, and any trained mage could tell.

There was something unusual – even startling – here, though, more so than a pointlessly levitating statue.

You could find raw magic everywhere in Agatos, and pretty much anywhere that a dead god had been worshipped. Perhaps there were a few distant mountain-tops or stretches of desert sand so remote from any god or their worshippers as to be free of it, but you could usually find at least a trace. If you wanted a really strong source of raw magic, the kind of power a high mage might be able to exploit, then your best bet would be to try to find a relic from a dead god. A fingernail or claw. A bit of hair. Anything you could get hold of and exploit the living – well, dead – shit out of. Me, I had no use for anything like that. I couldn't control anywhere near enough power to bother, and they weren't exactly selling godly relics on stalls at the Penitent's Ear.

Raw magic also tended to accumulate in artifacts associated with the god and in places of worship, like this temple. But I had never seen an accumulation of raw magic like this. The air inside the walls was thick with it, a shifting, swirling green that almost obscured my vision. It was unprecedented.

Yeah? And how much time do you spend in temples?

As little as possible, I had to admit. Maybe this often happened. It certainly explained the twirling statue. If the usual concentration of background raw magic was enough to keep it floating a hand's breadth above the altar and impress the worshippers, then this surge of raw magic had boosted it halfway to the ceiling and set it spinning.

I wondered if the temple had got hold of a relic of their god. But the raw magic didn't seem to be emanating from any particular location.

Sometimes levels of raw magic just fluctuated. I didn't know why. I guessed dead gods just rotted at different rates, or raw magic drifted like the smell of a dead fish on the breeze, sometimes faint, at other times overwhelming. Before long, this would probably fade, the statue would come back down, and everyone would go home disappointed and a bit poorer.

One thing I did know for sure: it really didn't have anything to do with me, and it wasn't going to come back to bite me. A shame I'd had to waste several coins to figure that out.

CHAPTER EIGHT

My intention had been to squirrel myself away at home and figure out how I was going to do what the smugglers wanted. How I could hide their unidentified, chest-sized magical item from view, what I could do if the plan exploded into shit like a blocked sewer after a storm, how I could signal Captain Gale without any accompanying smugglers noticing, and a hundred other details I wanted to nail down before I walked into this. But every idea I came up with brought another dozen complications, one after another, until I couldn't sit still.

Come on, Nik.

When a knock sounded at my door, I almost fell over my desk in my hurry to answer it. Maybe it was Captain Gale come to tell me she had nicked the lot of them after all, or the smugglers here to say they didn't need me and it had been a terrible mistake, or...

I flung open the door. The elderly man on the doorstep took a step back and almost toppled into the street.

"Mr. Inles?"

Bannaur's broken balls. My heart was rattling like a bird caught behind a window.

He tried a smile. It just looked guilty. "It's my dog. He's gone missing again."

Of course it had.

I stepped past him into the street and locked the door behind me with a quick spell. "Right. Come with me."

The smuggler was still watching my apartment from the other side of the street. It had done my heart good to see the expression on his face when I'd come back from Dumonoc's. *Didn't even realise I'd gone, did you?* I gave him a cheery wave.

Mr. Inles hurried to catch up. "Thank you. I couldn't find him anywhere. Do you know—"

I held up a hand. "Before anything else, we're going to buy you a leash."

It took most of the rest of the afternoon to track down his dog and then catch it, but I didn't charge him. I was grateful for the interruption, and I didn't think Mr. Inles had much else in his life.

Maybe I should get a dog, too.

"Just make sure you keep him on a leash when you take him out of your yard," I told him.

At some point during the afternoon, my smuggler had given up following me, the quitter. I took advantage of his absence to head out for an evening meal where I hoped no one would find me.

By the time I finally returned home, it was almost dark. I still hadn't figured out what I was going to do about the smugglers, but I operated better when I was making it up as I went along.

Yeah, you tell yourself that.

I wasn't at all surprised to see Dumonoc waiting outside my office.

"Are you ever in?" he grunted as I approached.

"Too busy out helping my appreciative customers."

"Fuck that. It's happening again."

I tilted my head.

"The curse. Bloke sent his drink back. Said it tasted off."

"Maybe he just had tastebuds."

"Funny. I kicked everyone out. Hurry up before it's too late."

I wasn't sure what I was supposed to do if the curse had already been laid. Save his stock, I supposed, but the evidence of the last few days suggested that was hardly a solution. At this rate, my fees would ruin him within the month. If he didn't give himself a heart attack before then. He looked like his blood vessels were about to burst.

"All right." I held out my hand, and he slapped a purse into it with a growl. Honestly, if it had been anyone else, I would have stopped charging until I had figured out who or what was behind it, but Dumonoc had spent the last five years insulting me, and this was just the world rebalancing itself. Who was I to argue with that?

Dumonoc's should have been busy at this time of night, but he hadn't been lying when he'd said he had kicked everyone out. He hadn't even let them finish their drinks.

I unfocused my eyes, and there it was again. The creeping, living curse, slipping over the drinks at one table and stretching tendrils out to wrap around neighbouring tables.

Dumonoc had caught it early this time. It hadn't had long enough to spread far. I broke the curse again and let it dissolve.

"Let's check the kitchen, too."

The kitchen was clean, as was behind the bar. There was no trace of the curse anywhere. Again.

"Right. Any of our suspects in since the last time I was here?"

Dumonoc shook his head. "Not even Squint."

Not a surprise. I hadn't thought they were behind it. "Tell me about the people who were at this table. Have you seen them before?"

"Yeah. But not in the last week. They don't come in often."

And who could blame them? "Did they upset anyone? Did they get into an argument? Did *you* piss them off?"

"Nah. *They're* not trouble." He raised his eyebrows. I chose not to notice.

"Whoever or whatever is causing this isn't going away," I said. "I think I need to stay here and keep an eye on things. I'll be able to catch whoever it is in the act." Then I could decide whether to slap them down or congratulate them.

"Fine." He would have sounded happier if he'd been chewing broken glass. "But you're buying your own drinks."

"I don't think so."

"I'm not a fucking charity."

"And I'm not drinking your drinks."

With that, I retreated into a corner, while Dumonoc took up position behind his bar, from where he glared at me like a badly-framed painting abandoned in a cellar. We would see which one of us lasted longest. I'd had practice.

After a few minutes, I said, "Aren't you going to open the bar?"

"What? And let some bastard come and curse me again?"

"You're planning to stay shut forever? I can hardly catch someone in the act if there's no one here, can I?"

Muttering to himself, Dumonoc unlocked the door. I took the opportunity to unfocus my eyes and check the place out. No curse yet. Good. Now I knew where we were starting from.

It didn't take long for the first customer to arrive, but the furious look on Dumonoc's face was enough to send her packing.

"And you say I scare off your customers."

Dumonoc didn't answer.

His regulars were less intimidated, and as the evening wore on, the bar slowly filled. Every few minutes, I unfocused my eyes and surveyed the space. A couple of customers had a low level of natural magical potential, but so minor that I doubted either they or anyone else had noticed. It wasn't the kind of ability that they would be able to do anything with, and it was common in Agatos.

"Something wrong with your eyes?"

I blinked and saw Squint, the information broker, leering over me, which was never a pleasant experience. The smell of stale wine and rotting teeth washed over me.

"You're a good one to talk." Squint hadn't come by his nickname by accident. Not for the first time, I wished someone would buy him a pair of glasses. Right after they bought him some false teeth to replace the brown stumps jutting from his gums.

He pulled out a chair. "Where's your wine?"

"You're going to have to buy your own tonight, Squint."

"Harsh. I've been hearing stories about you, Mennik Thorn."

He was fishing, and I wasn't biting. "Well, I hope they didn't keep you awake at night."

"Not me. I don't have nightmares. Word is, you might be having a bit of a nightmare yourself, though."

Nope. Still not biting. "I was fine until a couple of minutes ago."

"Ouch. That hurts my heart, that does."

"If you had a heart, you would have sold it ages ago. Now, if you don't mind, I'm working."

He perked up. "Really? On what?"

"Nothing you could sell. Now piss off."

I waited until he was seated at his usual table, then resumed my surveillance of the bar. Dumonoc's wasn't really the kind of place where people came to meet and chat. It was more the sitting-morosely-and-trying-not-to-have-to-drink-too-much-of-the-wine kind of place. Other than Dumonoc's insulting of the customers, it was hard to see what could have angered someone enough to repeatedly curse the place, and if you were a regular, you were used to the insults.

Maybe I had missed my chance. Maybe the curse I had broken earlier was it for the day. I was on the brink of telling Dumonoc that I would come back tomorrow when I realised something had changed. No one was using magic. No one was casting a spell or laying a curse. But the background raw magic was becoming stronger and more dense.

The magic in the Temple of Ethys had risen, too. Maybe it was happening all over Agatos. If so, I hadn't noticed it, and I didn't often see magic intensify so quickly. I waved Dumonoc over.

"Ready to buy a drink?"

I ignored that. "How far are we from the Temple of Ethys here?"

"How the fuck should I know?"

"It can't be more than a few blocks, right?"

"Fuck's sake. I have no idea."

I pushed up from my seat. "Wait here."

I heard him mutter, "Where the fuck did you think I was going to go?" as I headed out the door, up the stairs, and onto the plaza.

The raw magic was normal here, a thin green mist that I could see when I unfocused my eyes. It wasn't really a mist, of course. That was just the way that my brain interpreted it. Other mages interpreted magic in other ways, as sound or taste or sensation. Our brains weren't equipped to understand magic directly, so they resorted to involved metaphors. It allowed us a model to create spells, and at least I didn't feel like someone was poking needles in my skin or playing an out-of-tune violin in my mind, unlike some mages. Whichever way you sensed it, raw magic wasn't rising everywhere.

I checked the nearby alleys and the street behind Dumonoc's, but there was nothing unusual there either. Just at the temple and Dumonoc's.

I returned to the bar.

"I reckon raw magic is overflowing from the Temple of Ethys and erupting here," I told Dumonoc. I didn't know why or how, but there was a whole lot no one understood about how magic worked. Being able to grab hold and twist some of it into a spell wasn't the same as knowing what in the Depths you were grabbing or how it was grabbable. I had heard a bunch of theories in my time at Agatos University, but none of them had been convincing.

"That's what's causing the curse?"

"Well, no. Raw magic doesn't do anything by itself."

"Then why the fuck are you telling me? I have customers to serve."

Literally no one was waiting at the bar nor signalling for a drink, but it was a fair point. Raw magic wasn't his problem. Still, I couldn't believe it was unconnected. Maybe the sheer intensity of it had boosted the potential of some unknowing natural mage. I just ... didn't believe it. The curse had been complex. It hadn't been an accident.

I settled back and kept watching.

The raw magic intensified again. It seemed to be bubbling up in several different places, like water seeping through a crumbling dam. But, I had to remind myself, this was just the way my mind interpreted it. It wasn't flowing in a stream any more than it was a musical note heard in the distance or a drumming sensation on the skin.

The raw magic engulfed several tables and one end of the bar, but no one else seemed to notice. Even the patrons with natural magical ability didn't react, and the slow flow of magic they were absorbing didn't increase.

But then something did catch my eye. Unfolding from the air beside one of the tables, like a flower opening to the sunshine, was magic. A fine, organic magical structure, spreading itself through the raw magic, as though trying to engulf it.

No one was casting it. Casting a spell at a distance was tough, and even then, there would be a visible link to the mage responsible. There was nothing like that here. This thing was completely separate, almost as though it had poked through the fabric of reality to emerge like a butterfly from a chrysalis.

As its tendrils spread, it seemed to absorb and drain the raw magic. I hurried over.

"Shift," I told the man who was sitting at the table, hands wrapped around a cup of beer.

"What?"

"Shift."

The man eyed me, then got up with a curse.

"Leave your beer."

"Fuck you."

I pulled out a coin. "Buy yourself a new one."

With a shake of his head and some muttered words about how crazy I was, the man slouched his way to the bar.

I watched the magic unfold. It was definitely draining the raw magic from the room, growing as it did. Then, as the raw magic disappeared, the centre of the thing seemed to collapse as well, leaving only questing tendrils. I watched one of them wrap, net-like, around the abandoned beer, and I saw the beer turn foul.

There was magic in everything, particularly things that were alive or once had been. Food. Drinks that were made from grains or fruit. The remnants of this ... thing ... were drawing it from the beer, then spreading, reaching towards the nearby tables. A few tiny tendrils were even eating away at the wood of the furniture.

The thing that had caused it had disappeared along with the upwelling raw magic, but these remnants seemed determined to suck what remained from the food and drink. I was just grateful that it seemed unable to reach the raw magic inside living people. Mages couldn't do that, either, but this certainly wasn't being controlled by a mage.

In fact, I knew exactly what this was. I felt a grin start to spread on my face.

I broke the remnant magic, then hurried over to Dumonoc. "I know exactly what this is."

"I thought it was a curse."

"Nope."

"So what the fuck have you been charging me for?"

"It's called a Jaunt's Ghost. It's a magical phenomenon, maybe some kind of magical creature, that feeds on raw magic."

"I have no idea what you're talking about."

Right. Mages tended to remain tight-lipped about how magic worked, and most people didn't ask, wanting, quite rationally, to have nothing to do with mages or magic.

"You know sea anemones, right?"

"What the fuck do you think I am? You think I spend my days frolicking on the shore, crooning to gulls and playing tag with octopuses?"

Bugger me, but Dumonoc was hard work. And he wondered why more people didn't want to come to his bar. "But you know what they are. Think of a sea anemone on the edge of a tide pool."

"I have a bar to run, Thorn. I'm not here to listen to your stories. I would say you're drunk, except you haven't bought a single drink." He raised his eyebrows.

I ploughed on. "When the tide goes out and the anemone is left exposed, it looks dead. Just a brown lump on a rock. But when the tide come back in and submerges it, it opens up and starts waving its arms around and catching stuff. This is similar, except it's about magic, not water." When the concentration of raw magic grew high enough, this Jaunt's Ghost awoke and started feeding. It wasn't targeting Dumonoc's food and drink. That was just an after-effect, the last consumption of raw magic before it slipped completely into hibernation again. I had never seen one of these before. They were incredibly rare, to the extent that several academics argued they didn't exist at all. Finding one was ... exciting. I couldn't wait to tell, well, someone.

Not Dumonoc, though. "Whatever. Can you get rid of it? Kill it?"

"I'm not killing it." I didn't even know if it was alive in any meaningful sense. "And, no, I don't know how to get rid of it."

"Well, a load of fucking good you are. What a waste of my time."

I was tempted to leave it there and let Dumonoc's whole business crumble around him. No one could say he didn't deserve it. But, fuck it, I couldn't.

You never know when to walk away.

"I think I might be able to find out," I said.

CHAPTER NINE

I HAD READ ABOUT JAUNT'S GHOSTS DURING MY BRIEF TIME as a student at Agatos University. I had often retreated to the university library to avoid the other students. It had been that or vaporise the smug, arrogant bastards. To say I hadn't belonged with the scions of the privileged classes was like saying broken glass didn't belong in a bowl of stew. Not that any of them would have deigned to eat anything as common as stew.

It had been many years since I'd been a student. I had been expelled, but if I hadn't, I would have quit. I'd only been back once since, and it hadn't turned out well.

I hadn't been particularly interested in Jaunt's Ghosts when I'd come across them. They had been a passing curiosity in a book I flicked through. At the time, I'd been more interested in the history and secrets of the city. But if I was going to find out more, the university would be the best place to start. And at least it would take my mind off my coming showdown with the smugglers.

The university was a couple of miles north of the Grey City, following the river up through Agatos. It occupied a large campus on the eastern side of the valley, on the ill-judged bank of the Erastes river. Here, where the valley was relatively flat, the river flooded a couple of times a year, engulfing the ground floors of the closest buildings. You might have thought that a bunch of scholars would have noticed the potential for this when commissioning their buildings, particularly the second and third rounds of them, but only if you had never met any of the scholars. After a couple of hundred years sploshing around in cold water, they finally managed to overcome their stubbornness and made the radical decision to shift the colleges to higher ground, leaving only the youngest students to be regularly flooded out, on the dubious basis that they themselves had been flooded as students and it had never done them any harm.

The current library had been built further from the river and on higher ground, where it had sat unchanged and possibly undusted since. It was a grand building, somewhere between a palace and a temple, but with a very small door. The idea, I had once been told, was to symbolise the opening up of knowledge as you stepped through, but it just meant I banged my head half of the time. That probably symbolised something, too.

I set off early for the university, after only a couple of hours' sleep, to dodge both the heat and the scholars, who weren't known for starting early. I armed myself with my black cloak and reached the library before the last of the morning shadows had been chased from the steep-sided valley.

The tired scholar guarding the front desk of the library didn't look pleased to see me, but I raised a cheerful hand and headed past her for the stacks.

"Hold on," she called. "Are you a student here?"

Balls. I had thought that would work.

You're a mage. How would a mage act?

I strode over to the desk and looked down my nose at her. "The Countess" I said, letting contempt and an Upper City accent infuse my tone, "provides a generous endowment to the university. She would be very disappointed if she thought you were ungrateful."

All of which was true. My mother would be pissed off if one of her mages was denied entry. But I wasn't one of her mages, and she wouldn't give two fucks if I was kicked out on my arse. I was relying on my mage's cloak to sell this, so I gave it an unnecessary swirl. The scholar was young – the reason she was stuck with this unenviable duty – and she didn't know me, which was definitely to my advantage.

Her eyelid twitched, and she glanced around. There was no one else for her to turn to.

"Apologies, Mystery."

That was another thing I couldn't stand, their insistence on calling mages 'Mystery'. It managed to be both patronising and sycophantic simultaneously. I resisted the urge to tell her where to stick it.

It was strange being back here. I had still been one of my mother's junior acolytes when I had come to study here. By that point, she had decided that I did not, after all, have the potential to one day succeed her as High Mage. I suspected she had been grateful that I'd found an interest here. Perhaps she'd hoped I would obtain the skills to be useful to her in other ways. Being useful to her figured big in my mother's reckoning. But she had been wrong. It had been my first attempt, misguided though it was, to escape her influence. I hadn't fitted in here either, of course. I was temperamentally unsuited to being a scholar. Not long after my expulsion from the university, I had turned my back on the Countess for good and walked away to take up my life of success and fortune as a freelance mage.

Look how that had turned out.

Not much had changed about the library in my time away, certainly not the books. My new friend, Jettuk Kehsereen, whom I had met when he had drugged me, tied me up, and dumped me in an alley – an entirely innocent misunderstanding – was a scholar from the University of Khorasan, far to the north of the Erastes Valley. He had a very low opinion of the Agatos scholars, believing them to only endlessly recycle the opinions and discoveries of their predecessors, rather than researching anything new. He had a point, but it did mean that the library here had an enormous selection of texts spanning hundreds of years, even if many of them were shoddy, bigoted, and just plain wrong. Somewhere in here, if someone had learned the true nature of Jaunt's Ghosts, there would be a book describing it. The challenge would be to separate that from the reams of nonsense and ill-informed speculation surrounding it.

I found a well-concealed table, gathered books, and began my research.

Most scholars were not mages, which meant that while their discussions of history, politics, economics, arts, and sciences were generally well-informed – if occasionally quirky and stubborn – a lot of the material on magic, magical phenomena, and magical entities was little more than speculation, rumour, prejudice, and gossip. I worked my way through the stacks of books, discarding those whose authors were obviously talking out of their arses. After a couple of hours, I had reduced the piles to half a dozen volumes where the scholars at least seemed to understand how magic worked in practice. One of the authors, a Kallo Undrade, claimed to have been a mage in Hwat who had dedicated his life to studying magical phenomena. His book had an entire section on creatures that fed on raw magic. Life found a way, and if there was something that might possibly be eaten, something would arise that would eat it. We mages weren't the only ones to use raw magic.

Unfortunately, Undrade's text had been translated poorly from the original Middle Hwatian by someone who either wasn't a mage or spent a lot of time drunk.

Nonetheless, as I worked through the books, a few things became clear, or at least became a consensus. Jaunt's Ghosts were living creatures, even if they had no obvious physical body, and they were dormant when the levels of raw magic were low. So much, I had already concluded, although it was good to have it confirmed. The creatures consumed raw magic, then returned to dormancy, which explained why I hadn't been able to see the Jaunt's Ghost when the levels of raw magic were low, even though it was still there. The magic that I had seen eating through Dumonoc's food, drink, and even wooden furniture was indeed an after-effect of the creature's feeding. Undrade seemed to propose that this was in fact the creature's means of reproduction, and if high levels of raw magic returned while what I'd thought was a curse was still present, it would spawn more of the creatures. But the translator had either been very confused or very drunk during that passage, and it was hard to understand exactly what he was saying. Neither he nor any of the other writers said who Jaunt was nor why this 'ghost' was supposedly his.

It was also the case, several of the books seemed to agree – although I was starting to suspect that most of them were using Undrade as an uncredited source – that the more powerful the raw magic, the more destructive the after-effects. It was possible that Dumonoc's Jaunt's Ghost had always been there, but until this overspill of raw magic, its effects had been too mild to notice. And Dumonoc's drinks had always been terrible.

On how to get rid of the little bastards, well, the books were silent. Jaunt's Ghosts were often found where raw magic pooled – Undrade's word, not mine; or the word of his drunk translator, anyway. Again, not exactly news.

Or was it? Some materials could impede the flow of magic. Wood from an apple tree. Volcanic glass. Certain alloys. They were less effective against raw magic than structured spells, but even so, they would work well enough. Similarly, many crystalline materials could be used to store spells, while other materials seemed to act as a repository of raw magic, either because they had been imbued by a god's presence or because they naturally concentrated raw magic like a lens focusing sunlight.

I could try to cut Dumonoc's bar off from the raw magic spilling from the Temple of Ethys by lining the walls, floor, and ceiling of his bar with apple tree wood or volcanic glass. But that would be prohibitively expensive, and there was no guarantee it would work. A small gap – Depths, even the door – would let raw magic seep back in.

Well, how about if I got hold of some holy relic stuffed full of raw magic? I could attract the Jaunt's Ghost into it, leg it over to the Temple of Ethys, and dump it there. I couldn't deny that I would enjoy seeing the raw magic they were exploiting to pretend their god was about to return sucked away.

Yeah, and while you're at it, why don't you buy a palace up on Horn Hill?

Holy relics were incredibly expensive, both because temples could use them to bleed money from their worshippers and because powerful mages used them as repositories of power to draw on, and they were heavily protected. Benny had once swallowed a relic, a claw from the dead beast god Ah'té, just before its ghost could tear me to pieces. As far as I was aware, the relic had never ... come out the other end, so either it was still inside him or he had somehow digested it. Either way, my relationship with Benny right now wasn't such that I could ask to open him up and take a look.

So, maybe some material that could hold raw magic. If I could find a way to manipulate it into the material, it might become concentrated enough to attract the Jaunt's Ghost.

Might.

But what material?

I reached for another book.

"Well," a smug male voice said behind me. "This is a surprise."

I let my hand fall and swivelled in my chair.

There, dressed in the long, green robes of a scholar, was my former tutor from Pauper's College. "Scholar Longstream."

I hadn't had many lessons in Pauper's College, but when I had, it had always turned out to be this arsehole.

"Mystery Thorn. Imagine my surprise when a colleague told me they had seen you here. I had to come and see for myself. What exactly was it you said when we threw you out? I forget."

He hadn't forgotten at all. He remembered in perfect detail. "I said you were a bunch of stuck-up pricks who wouldn't know how the world really worked if it was shoved up your arses with a ten-foot pole."

"Up our arses. Ah, yes. Such a poetic turn of phrase. I assume, then, that you have not decided to re-enrol? After all, you were expelled. Perhaps" – he drew closer – "you have reconsidered my offer?"

"Your offer?"

"You remember. You came to me for help earlier this year. I offered you a deal. I believe you questioned my sanity."

"I said you were fucking crazy."

He had asked me to raise the dead body of the Godkiller, Agate Blackspear, the founder of the modern city of Agatos, and discover how Blackspear had killed Sien, the patron goddess of the city. It was possible to bring back the dead if you knew what you were doing. I had done it once only, when I had been training as a mage, and I had sworn I would never do it again. The dead always came back wrong, as though some essential part of them had been left behind, and it never ended well.

"You know Blackspear has been dead for four hundred years? All that will be left is some old bones. What do you expect? Him to clack his jaw bones at you?"

"I'm sure you could find a way."

"I was right. You are fucking crazy."

He straightened, offence twisting his lip. "Then I think you will have to leave. You do not belong here, Mystery Thorn. Go back to the gutter." He raised a hand, and two burly porters appeared from behind the stacks. Neither of them were mages. I could take them. But I had no issue with the university staff. Depths, I had been expelled in the first place for defending the staff against my fellow students.

"Fine. I'm done here anyway." I wasn't. I had wanted to research what materials I could use to hold raw magic. Preferably ones that wouldn't cost a fortune. That chance was gone. I grabbed my notes and tucked them inside my shirt. "I'm sure you can put the books back yourself."

CHAPTER TEN

My visit hadn't been a total disaster. I had confirmed my suspicions about the Jaunt's Ghost, and I had come away with an idea. More research would have been helpful, but I had picked up a few things during my mage training. Many crystalline materials, several metals, and a few other things could be imbued with spells. Mahogany was particularly good at anchoring wards, but I had a suspicion it didn't hold on to raw magic. Quartz was a jack-of-all-trades, and it had the advantage of being cheap and readily available, but it wasn't easy to imbue, and it didn't hold much. I would need a lot of raw magic for this. My best bet would be opal. It stored magic well and was quick to imbue and release. I hadn't had much opportunity to use opal – kind of out of my price range – but I thought it would work.

Of course, getting hold of a large enough opal wouldn't be easy. I wouldn't exactly find one lying by the roadside, and while I was doing all right, I certainly couldn't afford to buy gems. I could ask my mother or sister for help, but then I would have to explain all this, and I wasn't ready for that. It left me with only one real option: steal a fuck-off big opal.

Are you really about to risk that for bloody Dumonoc? He can't stand the sight of you.

And I couldn't stand the sight of him. But this had stopped being about Dumonoc some time back. I had made it my problem, and it would nag at me until I had dealt with the damned thing.

"Why do you do that, Nik?" I muttered to myself, startling an elderly man making his way back from the market. "Why do you have to take on the whole world's problems?"

I didn't answer. I just knew that if I tried to forget it, it would drive me mad.

You need help.

Maybe so. But what I really needed was a giant fucking opal.

I could only think of three places I might find a giant fucking opal: the palace of an incredibly rich merchant or Senator, of which there were several to choose from; a gem dealer; or one of the more prominent temples. Incredibly rich merchants and Senators also tended to employ incredibly powerful wards. Much of my mother's business involved creating these wards, and I was realistic enough to know that I couldn't break my way through. Gem dealers employed wards *and* guards. Big, tough bastards who didn't hang around to ask questions. I was handy enough in a street brawl, but I had no delusions about taking on a proper fighter, even if I did survive the wards. Which just left the temples.

Temples and money went together like a mage-for-hire and a free meal, and displaying their wealth was as natural to them as an exotic bird displaying its feathered arse to a potential mate. What their gods were supposed to do with all that money and all those jewels other than attract even more wealth was beyond me, but who was I to claim to know the minds of the gods, the grubbing little shits?

The Temple of Ethys was a no-go. With all the excitement from their floating statue, it would be too busy. If I'd been more religious, I might have had a better idea of which temples had opals in their collections. As it was, I had to do this the hard way: by foot. So, I headed for the Street of Gods.

The Street of Gods wasn't a street at all. It might have started out that way, but now it occupied a small district to the east of Horn Hill, just past the Agatos Arena. There were temples across Agatos, of course, from tiny, one-room shrines to gold-encrusted monstrosities like the Temple of Ethys, but in the game of 'my god is better than your god,' any priesthood who really wanted to challenge for the trophy had a presence in the Street of Gods. There was no shortage of religions in Agatos. Take your choice. From my point of view, they were each as useless as the next.

The first temple I came to was of Narth the Sleeping, but it turned out to be a bust. Their thing appeared to be rubies, glaring redly from the eyes of every non-sleeping statue. The Temple of the Third Apparition of Felen was too heavily guarded, and they were checking all their worshippers in and out. Maybe Felen had tipped them off about my plans.

I finally got lucky at a temple to Gwillan-Whose-Light-Falls-on-the-Few-Not-the-Many. Gwillan was a god of commerce and wealth, whose congregation was largely made up of merchants, and there wasn't a single merchant in the city who didn't enjoy parading their wealth in front of their rivals. Their god seemed to feel the same way, and I couldn't think of a more worthy god to steal from. After all, a priest of Gwillan had once stolen my ghost-hunting job when I'd needed it most. Admittedly, he'd then been ripped to shreds by the ghost of Ah'té instead of me, but it was the principle of the thing.

Gwillan's temple occupied a prominent position on the Street of Gods, opposite the gloomy Brythanii temple, a position not really in keeping with its small number of worshippers. Wide, gold-inlaid doors were warded against theft, because if there was one thing that Agatos could boast it was that someone would try to steal anything, no matter how large and inconvenient, if it was worth enough. No one wanted to come in for a quick morning's religioning and find their giant, solid doors had slunk off during the night.

The temple consisted of a central space and five spokes splaying outwards, representing the Five Virtues of Gwillan: greed, wealth, fucking over other people, and whatever the Depths the other two were. At the end of each spoke sat a statue of Gwillan, hands cupped, and in the palms of the leftmost statue was an opal twice the size of my fist. When I unfocused my eyes, I saw that I had been right. Raw magic was already dense within it. Maybe being a holy opal helped. The walls were hung with enormous tapestries, most showing scenes of merchants offering valuable gifts to the god. I had seen more subtle hints.

Now all I had to do was figure out how to make off with the opal in full view of the worshippers and priests. This was where Benny would have come in handy. I had tried not to ask too many details about Benny's career as a shameless thief. Now I was regretting that. I did know he spent several days scoping out a mark before he moved in. I didn't have time for that, and I didn't know what I should be looking for, anyway.

Perhaps I could create an illusion of the opal and swap that out for the real thing while I slipped away. It would be good practice for having to hide whatever magical item I was being forced to smuggle tomorrow night. If I couldn't distract a few dozen people from an opal, how would I keep the Warrens' criminal elements from seeing a large chest being carried by a band of smugglers?

"Nik?"

I started, almost dropping my mage's rod. While I had been staring at the opal like a complete idiot, a couple had walked right up to me.

"Mica?" My half-sister wasn't dressed like a mage, but she stood out anyway in her blue silk dress stitched with silver thread. "And ... um ..."

"Elestior," Mica's boyfriend – partner, whatever – said.

"Yeah. Right. Sorry." I hadn't forgotten his name on purpose, but something in my head kept trying to flush away his existence. He might not have been the privileged arsehole I had first assumed, but that didn't mean I had to like him. "What are you doing here? I thought you'd be up at Carn's Break with the rest of the..." I trailed off. Rich pricks, I had been about to say.

"Elestior is meeting with the head priest. We're hoping to get his support for a bill that we're pushing through the Senate."

"I thought you were all about helping the poor and downtrodden, not canoodling with the privileged."

Mica sighed. "You have to work with power to bring about the change you want, Nik. That's how politics works."

"Maybe you should just fuck them up until they do what you tell them." My sister was one of the most powerful mages in the city. As far as I knew, only our mother and the Wren could best her.

"And how do you think your friends in the Ash Guard would react to that? I was really hoping to live to a healthy old age." She leaned towards me. "Talking about the Ash Guard, there's a rumour going around that they want me to become a high mage. You haven't heard anything about that, have you?"

"No." I hadn't *heard*. It had been my idea, and I reckoned it was a pretty great one. "But, um, congratulations?"

"No. Not congratulations."

"You don't want the power and influence?" Being

declared high mage wouldn't make her a stronger mage, but it was a symbol. Other mages would flock to her cause. People would take note. She would *matter*.

"I don't want the attention. What Elestior and I are doing will only work if people don't see us as a threat. The moment everyone starts noticing us, it becomes ten times harder. The Wren and Mother will start to see me as a rival."

"Oh." Well, I had fucked that up, hadn't I? But I still stood by it. Captain Gale had made it clear that Agatos needed three high mages, so that no single high mage could hope to become dominant. Mica was the only candidate I trusted to really put the people of Agatos first, even if I wasn't sure about her methods. At least she meant well. "Maybe it's just a rumour."

"Maybe. But you tell me if you hear anything, right? I need to know."

"Sure." I smiled, and hoped I didn't look like a constipated seal.

"So what are *you* doing here, Nik? Don't tell me you're suddenly religious."

Stealing a giant fucking jewel. I bet that would go down well. "I'm working."

"At what?"

"That's confidential. I take my clients' privacy seriously."

She almost looked impressed.

I figured I should get out while I was ahead.

"Don't let me hold up your meeting," I said. "I'm done here, anyway."

~

I RETREATED TO A NEARBY COFFEE HOUSE SHADED BY A WIDE awning and several large, potted trees, which caught the faint, cooler breeze from the sea. I ordered an iced coffee and a cold cheese and spinach pie while I waited out the heat.

The priests weren't going to let me just walk in there and nick their giant and no doubt holy opal. Even if I managed to pocket it unnoticed, it would be pretty damned obvious it was gone and that the guy wandering away, whistling a jaunty and entirely innocent tune might have something to do with it.

I waved the waiter over. "Do you have a teapot? About this big?" I curled my hands in the air, fingertips an inch apart.

"You want some tea?"

"No. Just a teapot."

His forehead crinkled in confusion.

"Fine. Yes. Cardamom tea. In a pot that size, please."

I waited until he brought it and left again, then shuffled my body between the pot and the other customers. I carefully shaped a spell and laid it over the teapot. Not bad. The teapot now shone a deep, iridescent purple-blue.

Maybe too purple compared to the opal in the temple. I adjusted the spell. Yep. That would do it. I added some streaks of green and yellow. From a distance, you could easily mistake this for an opal. Although it would be more convincing without the spout and handle.

Of course, a mage would be able to tell right away, and while I didn't expect to run into another trained mage like my sister at the Temple of Gwillan-Whose-Light-Falls-on-the-Few-Not-the-Many, some priests were definitely mages, particularly those who worshipped dead gods. A priest of a living god might be able to resort to bribing, badgering, or arse-kissing their god into a minor miracle. Priests of dead gods didn't have that luxury. All they had was access to an abundant supply of raw magic. They might not call themselves mages, and they might not have the same training, but if you manipulated raw magic, that made you a mage, even if you did it in robes with bells and smoke.

Gwillan was a living god, and I had seen one of his priests produce a miracle. Not that it had helped him. He had been meat, blood, and piss on the floor moments later. But it had been a proper god-given miracle. Mages were less common in temples to living gods – see the 'minor miracles' get-out clause – but they weren't unknown. Sometimes it was easier to cast a quick spell to impress your congregants than to persuade an arsehole god to do you a favour. All-in-all, it would be better if none of them saw me working magic.

I stayed in the coffee house until the city started to grow dark. Whatever meeting Mica and Elestior had been involved in would be long over by now.

I beckoned the waiter over one last time. "I'll be keeping the teapot."

He started to frown again, and I dropped a silver watchman on the table. He snatched it up with a shrug. I was going to go broke at this rate.

Carefully, I snapped off the handle and the spout and left them beneath one of the potted trees, then headed back to the temple.

At this time of year, Agatos came alive in the cooler hours of the evening and night, but the same couldn't be said for the Temple of Gwillan. I put it down to a combination of devotees not wanting to waste the tolerable temperatures religiousing, the temple itself being relatively cool during the day, and many of the wealthiest merchants being off at Carn's Break. A good part of the motivation of coming to the Temple of Gwillan in the first place was to rub shoulders with other, more successful merchants and make connections. Even so, the temple wasn't completely empty. A dozen worshippers and as many priests were engaged in their rituals, which seemed to involve a lot of bobbing up and down like gulls on a stormy sea, including a group in front of my statue. The opal was about twelve feet up, then a scramble along the arms of stone Gwillan. I wasn't going to manage that unobserved.

So, get rid of the priests and worshippers, grab the opal, leave the teapot, and head out before anyone noticed.

Easier said than done. Perhaps I should just knock out this little group. Which would be great until someone wandered past and noticed a heap of bodies and one awkward mage dangling from the stone arms of a giant statue.

A distraction. Benny had always said I was good at causing chaos, and I had made it my signature move. My *fucksthat* spell was one of my proudest achievements. It was an illusion that consisted of rainbow-coloured explosions, accompanied by unearthly screams, a wild storm wind, and dark, demonic figures hauling their way out from the depths of the earth. None of it was real, of course, but it would absolutely get everyone's attention.

Unfortunately, it was so vigorous that it would draw gawkers from the street outside, and I would be risking more eyes on my antics. I might also have used it too much, and people – including the Watch – were starting to associate it with me. That was the problem with a signature move.

I would save it for tomorrow night's excitement with the smugglers if Captain Gale's plan went wrong. Tonight I needed something more subtle.

The final spoke on the opposite side of the temple was empty. If I'd wanted to steal a diamond worth more than the street I lived on, it would have been the perfect opportunity, but diamonds were weak reservoirs of spells and actively repelled raw magic. I would have had more luck with a cobblestone from the street outside.

Time for a classic.

I gathered as much raw magic as I could hold, shaped it to a point, and released it into a bench at the far end of the spoke, just to one side of the diamond-holding statue. The wood burst into flame, and I controlled the temperature of the fire until smoke billowed out like steam from a kettle. I could have done it as an illusion, of course, but then the first person to get a lungful of 'smoke' or toss water onto the fire would unmask it right away.

And it was only one bench. They could afford a new bench.

I waited until the smoke was pouring out and filling the air, then I shouted, "Fire! Help! Fire!"

If there was one word guaranteed to cause people to start running in every direction, it was 'fire'. Within moments, the temple was a chaos of fleeing worshippers and wildly flapping priests. I was quite satisfied by the whole thing. I headed towards my target.

So, up the statue, along its arms... Fuck that. Close up, the statue was far bigger than I had thought. I still had some sense of dignity, and the idea of being caught trying and failing to scramble up there or falling off and knocking myself unconscious ... no thanks.

I checked the chaos behind me. I had done a great job with the smoke. It was really pumping out. I took a breath, focused on the orb, and reached towards it with magic. Then I lifted.

Or I would have. But nothing happened. The opal stayed put. I fed in more magic and heaved. Still nothing.

The untrusting bastards had fixed it in place. I strained with the spell, but I couldn't shift it. If I put in more power without being able to see what I was doing, I would shatter the gem.

The smoke was growing thicker. I breathed in a lungful and coughed. How in the Depths had one bench produced so much smoke? My spell had been way more effective than I had imagined. And people said I was a shit mage.

If I wanted to keep breathing, I was going to have to speed this up. So much for subtlety.

I pulled in raw magic again, refocused it into a sharp wedge, and split the statue at its wrists. The sandstone cracked with a satisfying explosion, spraying shards of stone onto the marble floor. The stone hands dropped with a sound like a cannonball hitting a cliff.

I spun again, but the temple was half full of smoke, and no one was paying me any attention.

Maybe I *had* been a little bit overenthusiastic with the distraction.

I hurried over to the stone hands. The opal still sat cupped in them. It was clasped in a claw-like cage of iron that I hadn't been able to see from below. The iron claws had left scratches on the surface of the opal as I had tried to tug it free. I'd been lucky it had survived.

Now that I could see what I was dealing with, it was easy enough to lever the claws apart.

There you are. An opal this size would hold a good reservoir of raw magic. *Enough to attract a Jaunt's Ghost?* We would see.

And if you don't get out of here soon, you know you're not going to see anything at all. This smoke couldn't all be coming from one bench. I removed the teapot from inside my shirt, placed it in the broken-off hands of the statue of

Gwillan, cast my spell on it, then inspected my work. Not bad. Maybe it wouldn't stand up to a close inspection, but at a glance it looked like a large opal. I tucked the real opal into my shirt, my shirt into my trousers, tightened my belt enough to stop myself breathing, then legged it.

As I ran past, I saw the fire had spread from the bench to engulf several large tapestries on the wall, and the flames were now running like fingers over the wooden beams that supported the roof.

You realise you're burning down a temple to help Dumonoc? You don't even like Dumonoc.

I burst out the doors in a belch of smoke, head ducked, then slipped away through the excited crowd of spectators before the Watch could arrive.

No one looked at me as I went. It was fully dark now, and although there were morgue-lamps on the Street of Gods, I was just another hurrying figure. With the thrill of a burning temple to distract them, no one would remember a tall mage who had been in the temple at the time. I wondered what Benny would think about my escapade. He would probably be appalled at my incompetence.

Not that you'll get a chance to tell him. The reminder that I had fucked up my oldest, best friendship made my whole body tighten in a way that the disastrous burglary hadn't. *Nothing you can do about it now.*

I should get the opal back home, see if I really could stuff it with raw magic, then head to Dumonoc's and try to deal with the Jaunt's Ghost. Tomorrow night, the smugglers would have me, and if it all went wrong – *when* it all went wrong – I might not get a chance to do anything else ever again. I didn't like the idea of leaving this hanging. I couldn't fix my friendship with Benny before then, but maybe I could do this. It was a poor substitute.

Like you're going to care one way or the other if you've got a brain full of bullets.

I was tired. I hadn't done much today, but I was tired anyway. I always preferred my disasters to catch me unawares. When I knew they were coming, the stress built up. Better not to know and just react.

I cut through the Penitent's Ear market, then across a couple of streets until home was in sight. Maybe a few hours' sleep before trying the opal would help.

For once, Dumonoc wasn't waiting on my steps. I climbed wearily to the door, unlocked it, stepped into my office, and stopped.

The leader of the smuggling gang was sitting behind my desk, pistol levelled at me.

CHAPTER ELEVEN

I STARTED TO THROW UP A SHIELD BEFORE REALISING THAT the smugglers' leader wasn't alone. Stationed around the room were another half-dozen men and women, and every one of them had a gun.

I could take them, I reckoned, at least long enough to get away. But then what? I would still be on the run. I would still have to watch my back every moment of every day.

My only way out of this was to deal with the whole gang in one go, and for that, Captain Gale's plan was still my best bet.

"What do you want?" I demanded. "I said I would be ready tomorrow, and I will be."

The smuggler smiled. "You must think I am a fool."

My heart stuttered. Did she know about my meeting with Captain Gale? Had I been followed after all?

"I have no idea what you're talking about."

She shifted, her heavy jewellery clacking like teeth, but her pistol remained steady on me. "I do not trust you, mage. Did you really think I would tell you exactly when we were bringing our cargo in?"

"I don't understand."

"It is tonight, not tomorrow night."

Bannaur's balls!

"It can't be. I've got to... I need to..." What? What excuse could I give? *I've got to warn the Ash Guard?*

She waved her pistol, and I resisted the urge to duck.

"Move."

Shit and fuck and bloody Depths! I was buggered. Truly, painfully screwed. My only hope of getting out of this had been Captain Gale's carefully laid plan, which wasn't happening for another full day. Screwed.

"You can leave that," she said, nodding at my mage's rod.

I shook my head. "Can't do magic without it." A complete lie, of course. If all else failed, I intended to brain some fucker with it.

"Then I'll carry it." She held out a hand. Reluctantly, I passed it over.

I allowed myself to be ushered out and onto the street. Guns disappeared beneath cloaks, but I was painfully aware that they were still there. I could also feel the cold bulk of the opal beneath my shirt. I tugged my own cloak around to hide it.

We headed down into Dockside, then through the

narrow streets and along the shadowed docks, cutting east across the face of the city, before crossing the Erastes River at the Wet Bridge and looping up and around to skirt Fishertown. Fishertown was a close, insular community, and smugglers weren't welcome there. Maybe I could do something with that information. I just didn't know what.

At the point where the Ependhos Mountains that formed the eastern wall of the valley sliced down to meet the sea, a jagged, rocky outcropping jutted over a mile into the bay to enclose most of the harbour. This was the Dragon's Jaw. Whether it was a natural feature or it had been created by an over-exuberant mage, I didn't know. But, along with the western sea wall, it formed a formidable defence against attack from the sea. Gun emplacements every hundred yards along its length, coupled with a low wall and a precipitous drop to the waves below, would make it a near-impossible target, but it had been hundreds of years since anyone had tried, and the Dragon's Jaw was more popularly used for fishing from the rocks. Not tonight, though. Some sense of self-preservation – or just direct threats – had cleared the night fishermen.

The Dragon's Jaw met the land just above Fishertown. Here, access to the outcropping was controlled by a small fort, although the gate had been left open for as long as I could remember. I thought about calling to the soldiers stationed there as we passed through, but the same questions remained: what then?

Captain Gale was right – frustratingly, she was almost always right. The smugglers had to be caught in the act, all of them. And Captain Gale and her squad weren't expecting us until tomorrow night.

Somehow, I needed to get a message to her. My *fucksthat* spell would draw attention. But it would take Captain Gale too long to assemble a squad and charge down to the docks. I might last a minute or two, but twenty minutes? Half an hour? I didn't think so.

I felt my vision closing in, my heart rate speeding up, hot and cold chasing across my skin like a fever.

You've been in worse situations like this. You've survived.

And how many times can you toss the coin and have the lady come face up?

My luck wouldn't last forever.

So, go through with it. Look for an opportunity to get word to Captain Gale or leave a signal pointing to wherever they were planning to hide this magical item. Don't do anything stupid.

I forced my breath to slow.

About half way along the Dragon's Jaw, the smugglers' leader came to a halt and scrambled up onto the wall that ran along the ocean side of the Jaw. "It's here," she called back. "Come on."

One of the smugglers gestured with his gun – the guns had come out again when we had started along the outcropping – and I pulled myself up beside her.

Beyond the Jaw, the near-black waters of the Erastes Bay heaved weightily. They looked alive, like a slow, ancient beast shifting in its sleep. Moonlight wrote lines across the tops of the waves. I had never liked the ocean, and in the dark, I liked it even less. Below us, a small boat was tied against the rocks. It looked frail and ridiculous on the surface of the water, as though it would take almost nothing to pluck it up and flick it across the waves.

A rope had been tied to a metal ring just below the wall, trailing down to the boat.

"Are you taking the piss?" I was supposed to – what? – swing over the edge and climb down that? The temptation to sweep her off the wall with my magic was almost overwhelming.

The smuggler's eyes hardened. She poked her pistol into my side, close to the awkwardly hidden opal. "Down there, mage."

"Fine. Keep your hair on." I didn't want her discovering the opal. After all I'd gone through to get it, I wasn't having her nicking it.

Like you're going to get a chance to use it.

I moved to the edge of the wall. Shit, it was a long way down. I lowered myself into a crouch, then clumsily slid over the side so that I was only holding myself by my bent arms. *Denna's mercy.* I was going to kill myself. My legs kicked hopelessly in the air.

Now how are you going to get hold of the rope, you twat?

I risked turning my head and peered down. Oh, shit. A thirty-foot fall to jagged rocks, maybe more.

Calm. Breathe.

I stilled my legs. *There.* Just to the right, a rock poked out. I shuffled across until I got my foot on it. That was better. At least it took some weight from my shoulders. I licked my lips, then let go with one hand and reached for the rope.

My foot slipped. My weight dropped, my remaining arm came loose, and I fell.

I snatched the rope.

The fibres burned my skin. The jolt almost dislocated my shoulder. I thumped into the cliff, smacking my head. I felt the opal slip and slapped my free hand against it.

I hung there for a second, until I was sure the opal was safe. Then, finally, I got my other hand on the rope, braced my feet on the uneven rocks, and slowly lowered myself down to the boat.

Every part of me hurt. My arms, my hands, my body, and my head where I had slammed into the rocks. I watched bitterly from the boat, hands clasped on the gunwales, as the smugglers easily followed me down. Maybe if one of them had gone first, I would have seen how to do it.

From where we were, I couldn't see the ship we were supposed to be meeting. The sky was clear, stars glittering and sharp, but the long, deep-ocean waves dipped us and dropped us, and in their blackness, they could be hiding a hundred equally black ships.

I tried to steady myself as the smugglers cast off the boat, picked up the shipped oars, and began to drive us out onto those empty waves. I wondered if they intended to tip me overboard when we were far enough out and let me drown.

Why would they? They could have shot you any time.

I couldn't push away the sensation that we were balanced precariously above a great height and at any moment we might plunge down, like the boat was suspended by ignorance alone above the blackness of the sky.

"You're not much of a sailor, are you?" the smugglers' leader said in a low voice, to the sounds of quiet laughter from the other smugglers.

"Yeah, well, you're not much of a mage," I said through gritted teeth.

Agatos was unbearably hot at this time of year, even at night, but out in the bay, the ocean drew heat from my skin, and the breeze sent chills across my body. Water slapped like hands on the boat.

From here, the Dragon's Jaw blocked the sight of the lower city, but the lights of the Upper City and Horn Hill bobbed like drunken constellations. Captain Gale had said there could be a dozen ships waiting out here in the bay, but I couldn't see them, and we were as alone out here as we would have been in the middle of a desert. The smugglers rowed on confidently.

At least they know where they're going.

I hoped. Speaking for myself, I was capable of heading in the wrong direction with great confidence.

But the smugglers were either competent or lucky, and within an hour, the bulk of a ship resolved out of the darkness.

Minutes later, we came alongside, oars were re-shipped, a ladder thrown down, and the smugglers swarmed up to the deck above. I followed shakily. I didn't care that I was far slower. Even though I hadn't rowed, I felt weak from the trip across the water.

Not my element. Even though Agatos was a port city, most of us who lived there never ventured into the bay.

Hands pulled me onto the deck. I turned to look back at the land. The lights of Agatos seemed so faint and distant, almost an illusion. I saw about a dozen sailors on deck, as well as the smugglers who had accompanied me. The sailors were going about their work, deliberately not paying attention to us. They must know what was going on, must be in the pay of the gang, at the very least, but I could have learned a lesson from them: don't stick your head in where it's not invited.

"I assume you're prepared?" the smugglers' leader said, coming up beside me.

"I would have been prepared tomorrow night," I said. "Which was when I was expecting to have to do this." Prepared to bring the Ash Guard down on them like a herd of angry bulls.

Her eyebrows rose.

"I need to see what I'm protecting if this is going to work," I said. "You haven't given me much to go on."

I wasn't lying. It would be hard enough if I was prepared. Coming in cold, I would have no hope. Not that I wanted it to get that far. I wanted a whole squadron of Ash Guard lined up along the dockside when we stepped off the ship.

And how are you going to achieve that?

The smuggler eyed me thoughtfully, then nodded. "Follow me."

She led me below deck, down a steep wooden ladder. Only a couple of dim oil lamps shone in the crew's quarters. The ceiling was too low for me, hammocks slung like shadows across the space, swinging gently, and more were tied back. Snores rose from the occupied hammocks.

How in all the Depths could they sleep on this bloody fragile wooden construction? *No. Don't call on the Depths out here.* How the *fuck* could they sleep?

I estimated another couple of dozen sailors down here. A couple more watches. A lot of them, even without the smugglers who had followed me down. I wasn't going to fight my way out of this.

And where would you go, anyway? Into the water? That little boat? And swim or row back to shore? I wouldn't make it. *Just find out what you're dealing with first.* Then maybe – maybe – I could figure out some way of contacting Captain Gale. Maybe I could send a magical message to my sister. I hadn't done that for years, and never from this far. I hadn't wanted to touch the thoughts of another mage, even before I had struck out on my own. When you opened yourself up like that, other thoughts leaked through.

What's better? To trust the smugglers not to knife you in the back or to let Mica into your head? She was my sister. She wouldn't pry.

Yeah? And you wouldn't pry into her thoughts if you had the chance?

That was different. She was a better person than I was.

You sure? You hardly know her anymore.

Maybe it wouldn't come to that.

The air was stale down here. Sweat, old breath, oil from the lamps, and oily smoke. At least I didn't get seasick.

We made our way between the swaying, sleeping bodies. I kept my head down to avoid banging it on the heavy wooden beams above me.

Eventually, we reached a door at the back of the cabin. The smugglers' leader rapped on it three times, then waited a few seconds and opened it.

Two more smugglers waited in the storeroom beyond, both armed, flintlock pistols pointed at the door. The room held several barrels, sacks, and chests. I could smell tea and spices. If this was their valuable cargo, I was going to be truly fucking disappointed.

"Open it," the smugglers' leader said.

The men moved aside a sack, then levered away the planks of the wall behind. *Clever.* A hidden compartment. If the ship was inspected, it would take a pretty thorough search to find this.

Perhaps the ship would be searched after all. A customs boat meeting it as it sailed in. Maybe I would be able to pass a message.

That's not how it works. The customs agents wouldn't send a boat out in the deep of the night. They would come to where it was moored in the morning.

The two smugglers reached in and drew out a sturdy chest. It looked heavy and solid. I wouldn't be able to grab it and run. They placed it on the floor and stepped back, nodding.

I made to reach for it, but the smugglers' leader closed a hand around my arm. She had a strong grip.

"Look. Don't touch."

Fine. I would look. But not like this.

"I'm going to need that." I indicated my mage's rod.

She lifted it, considering. "As you wish." She glanced at the other smugglers. "Watch him closely."

CHAPTER TWELVE

WITH THE HEAVY WEIGHT OF THE ROD IN MY HAND, I FELT more confident. Knowing I could crack someone's skull if it came to it cheered me up. I unfocused my eyes.

The chest was shielded, I could tell that straight away. There was a certain quality to the raw magic that seeped from it – a uniform mistiness. It was probably made of apple tree wood, and what was within was a source of raw magic, as I had expected. Perhaps an artifact from the temple of a dead god.

That wasn't so bad. It was powerful enough that the apple tree wood allowed raw magic to pass through, but not unusually so. I could see why a mage would want to buy it. It wouldn't be much use to me. My limitation wasn't the amount of raw magic I had access to. It was an inability to channel large quantities of power without ripping myself to pieces. A more potent mage engaged in a serious piece of magic might find the ambient raw magic around them running short. Having access to their own private source could be incredibly useful. I knew my mother had several, as did Mica and undoubtedly the Wren. What did it matter if another high-powered mage had easier access to power?

Ordinary mage activities weren't illegal. The city's quarries used a lot of mage power to bring down and shape slabs of rock. At some point, the bottom of the harbour had been scraped out of the bedrock with vast amounts of magic. This wasn't necessarily a bad thing. Yeah, it should have been legally imported, but I wasn't putting my neck on the line so the city could grab a chunk of taxes.

It wasn't like they could do anything bad with it, not unless they wanted the Ash Guard up their arses like a swarm of furious hornets.

And that, that there, was me trying to fool myself, even though I knew better.

If there's power there, they'll use it, and not for anything good. If whoever was buying it wanted it for a legitimate reason, they would have bought it legally. These last few months had taught me that a lot of people might die before they were stopped.

And what if it's not an artifact? What if it's something else? Something even more dangerous.

You need to check.

Fuck. Why couldn't I just go along with it? Why couldn't I convince myself? This was none of my business. My only business was getting out of this alive. I could figure out how to get the smugglers off my back another time. I didn't hold any of the cards here.

"You done?" the smugglers' leader demanded.

I shrugged. "I'm going to have to do some work. Whatever is in there is leaking magic. A mage would see it. I'm going to have to find some way to obscure it."

"Hurry it up. We'll be docked in an hour. Then we move. We won't have time to waste." She leaned close. "If you fail, we will kill you."

"Yeah. You made that clear." I looked up at her. "You know that at some point threats lose their impact? Just give me some time and space here."

Her gaze dwelled on me, then she nodded again. "If he tries anything stupid, shoot him. Somewhere that will hurt. I need him alive. I don't need him happy."

No danger of that.

I settled back and eyed the chest. The raw magic wasn't leaking from any particular flaw. That would have been easy to fix. Instead, it was diffusing through the wood. Carrying it through the streets of the city would be a beacon to every mage nearby, and I knew the Wren, at least, had mages watching the lower city. My mother no doubt did the same, and I knew mages. The smugglers had offered this item for sale, and every mage they had told about it would now be on the lookout for a chance to steal the damned thing. Somehow, it had become my job to stop that happening.

Every mage manipulated raw magic in order to create spells. But I wasn't looking to draw in the raw magic. What

I needed was to figure a way to trap the raw magic inside the chest, at least for long enough to get it into hiding. Manipulate it back into the chest before it could properly emerge. It would be good practice for squeezing raw magic into my opal. If I survived long enough to do that.

The two smugglers staring at me weren't helping me concentrate.

"So," I said. "Been smuggling long?"

"Just do your job," one of them grunted, the bigger of the two. He was Mycedan, like most the gang. His blue tattoo looked painfully close to his eye. No wonder he was bad-tempered.

"How do you know I'm not?" I waggled my fingers, and he flinched back, then lifted his pistol. I put up a shield in case he was jumpy, but a moment later, he lowered the gun.

"I could really do with a look inside that," I said, nodding at the chest.

"No chance. Boss's orders."

What the fuck was *in* there? It made a difference, but more than that, I felt an overwhelming compulsion to *know*.

This is how you get in trouble.

I moistened my lips, then reached for the raw magic leaking from the chest. Habit tugged it towards me, like water running downhill. I had trained to do this for so many years the instinct was almost irresistible, like breathing.

I shut out the sounds around me, the creaking of wood, the shouts from the deck, the swish and rush of water over the hull, the breathing of my guards. I pushed away the slow rocking of the ship. This wasn't so different to casting a spell at a distance, something that many mages couldn't pull off, but which I had learned to do years ago. Both meant manipulating magic away from my centre, where I had first learned to trap and change it.

But this wasn't a spell. This magic wasn't *mine* yet. I hadn't taken it and formed it.

If you can pull, you can push.

Maybe that was the way to do it. I let my instinct pull the raw magic from the box towards me, then shoved. The raw magic swirled like ink in water.

Good. That had worked. Now what?

Constrain it somehow. Don't push so hard. Push from every side.

I let my breath settle again. This was difficult. Now I wished I'd studied more. I knew mages manipulated raw magic. But what exactly were we doing? How did our will take raw magic and move and change it? That would be very fucking useful to know right now.

You work with what you know.

All right. I pulled raw magic towards me from the chest, then pushed again, but this time from the sides, above, and below, as well as from in front. The pressure in my head felt like a nosebleed. Again, the magic swirled, but this time it was constrained. I kept hold of it and pushed harder, forcing it back towards the chest.

Something trickled over my lips. I tasted it. Yep. Blood.

The raw magic encountered resistance as I pushed

against the apple tree wood, compacting on the outside like thick smoke.

I shoved with sudden force. For a second, I thought it would work. Then the raw magic burst free, spiralling through the air and dissipating.

Shit!

That apple tree wood was too much of a barrier, and the raw magic too hard to grasp.

I drew a sleeve across my face, wiping away the blood. My head wanted to explode.

I blinked and noticed the two guards gaping at me.

"This isn't easy," I said.

So, forcing the raw magic back into the chest wasn't possible. Maybe I could stop it coming out in the first place. I focused. My mouth was dry, my heart pounding.

Calm. This was just magic. It wasn't like my life was at stake or anything.

I ignored the raw magic that had leaked from the chest. Instead, I imagined a flat barrier pushed right up against the surface of the wood, then held it there as tightly as I could. I had no idea what I was pushing *with*. My imagination, I supposed. I knew that raw magic wasn't, objectively, a green mist, so I couldn't actually be pushing against it. If I had sensed magic as music, what would I be imagining instead? Some counter melody cancelling it out?

Focus!

Bannaur's balls, this was difficult. The raw magic was a constant pressure. What the fuck was in that chest?

No. It still wasn't working. My barrier was stopping the

raw magic, but it was condensing like a glowing sheet of paper on the outside of the chest.

I let it go. The raw magic dissipated again.

Fuck! If I could just get into that chest, maybe I could put a barrier around the artifact itself rather than trying to deal with the magic after it had escaped.

I eyed the smugglers. No. They were not going to be helpful. I could see the sullen stubbornness in their faces. Probably why they'd been chosen as guards.

"Good job, is it, smuggling? Taking things in and, er, taking things back out again?"

"Shut up."

Delightful. I straightened. "I'm going to need you out of here for this next part."

The smugglers exchanged glances. "No. Boss's orders. We stay."

It was like talking to a pair of planks. "Fine. You probably didn't want kids anyway, right? In your job."

"What?"

"You probably don't have much use for what's down there." I indicated my groin and waggled my eyebrows.

Nothing. Denna's mercy, these two were dumb. I started my hands glowing. Was that a flicker in the right one's eyes? They still weren't moving, though. Either they saw through my goat shit or they were terrified of their leader. Well, I wasn't finished yet.

"Just remember," I said. "This was your choice."

I formed magic again, concentrating heat on both of their groins, slowly increasing it.

For a couple of seconds, they toughed it out – impressively long, really – as I brought the temperature uncomfortably high. Then one of them shouted, “Fuck this!” and they were both heading for the door.

I wouldn’t have long. The moment they found their leader, she would be back here with guns, and I would have to fight or give in. I didn’t fancy fighting my way off the ship in the middle of the ocean.

I wouldn’t *need* long. Find out what I was dealing with, see if I could suppress or contain the raw magic. That was all. Then I could decide what to do next.

I knelt in front of the chest and placed my hands on either side of the lid. It was locked, but that wasn’t a problem. I’d had a lot of practice with other people’s locks, and this was nothing special.

Carefully, ready to counter or dodge any booby traps set for inquisitive mages, I lifted the lid.

I wasn’t faced with an old artifact from a temple, imbued with the borrowed essence of a dead, rotting god, nor with an artificial reservoir of power like I intended my opal to become. Instead, a solid block of volcanic glass glistened up at me. I stared at it, confused. You couldn’t imbue magic in volcanic glass, even raw magic. The substance repelled magic like a drop of water on oil.

I unfocused my eyes. The raw magic was seeping through the volcanic glass. *Through the fucking volcanic glass!* My fingers twitched involuntarily. Even a high mage couldn’t push magic through volcanic glass.

You’ve seen something like this before.

All the sounds of the ship had disappeared. All I could hear was the blood beating in my ears.

I had found a box lined with volcanic glass in a warded safe owned by the renegade mage Enne Lowriver. It had been empty when I'd found it, but it had been used to store a claw from her dead beast god, Ah'té. She had used the power within it to raise ghosts around the city and summon the spirit of her dead god. That box had been not much bigger than my two spread hands, and I had lifted it easily. This chest was ten times the size, and it had taken two men to lug it out.

I released a slow breath. Ah'té's claw was gone. Benny had swallowed it, that daft bastard. This wasn't it.

Licking my dry lips, I reached into the chest. The block of volcanic glass wasn't completely solid. Looking closer, I could see a horizontal line around it. A chest within a chest. I gripped it, slowed my breathing, and lifted.

The lid was heavy. I had to strain to lever it off. It was almost as though there was a vacuum inside, holding it tight. With a wrench, I jerked it free. It tumbled to the planks with a crash.

It took me a second to realise what I was looking at.

There was a foot inside the box. A hollow had been carved from the volcanic glass, and the foot lay in it, cleanly severed at the ankle. It wasn't just an ordinary foot. It was fucking enormous. My feet were pretty big, but this one was three times the size.

Good luck finding shoes for that.

Nervously, I unfocused my eyes.

Raw magic blazed from it like a waterfall of green light, spraying out in every direction. It burned into my retinas like I was staring at the midday sun. I staggered back, arm coming up, and blinked my eyes into focus.

Bannaur's bleeding balls!

I slammed the volcanic glass lid back on. My heart was pounding, cold sweat soaking my skin. *Fuck!*

This wasn't just an artifact. It was the foot of a goat-fucking dead god.

CHAPTER THIRTEEN

My mind didn't want to accept it. A foot. A whole Cepra-damned foot.

Maybe that didn't sound like much, but a single fingernail would be enough to provide all the power a high mage would need. This ... this was a tidal wave crashing down on the city. Worse. A significant portion of a dead god's potency was sitting in this chest.

Fuck knows what the Wren or the Countess could do if they got hold of this.

Or one of the pretenders to the vacant High Mage position.

The balance in the city was a delicate one, even when there were three high mages. Only the knowledge that an outright confrontation would do them irreparable harm kept them from each other's throats. But with this? It would throw that balance so far off that the rest of the city would come tumbling down.

The Ash Guard would stop it. No matter how powerful a mage was, they couldn't overcome Ash, and I knew Captain Gale. She would come with Ash smeared on her face and skin, sword in hand, and that would be the end of the high mage or the pretender.

If she knows who has it. If they act openly. The Wren and the Countess were clever. If they got it, they would wait, and when they struck, they would make sure it couldn't be tracked back to them. The Ash Guard required proof. I had found that to both my benefit and detriment over the last few months. When the smugglers sold it, the foot would disappear until it was time for the mage to make their move.

I cracked open the lid again. Raw magic blazed like a beacon.

What in the Depths was I supposed to do?

The Depths. That was it. I could drop it overboard, into the ocean depths. Sealed in volcanic glass and apple tree wood and far below the waves, no one would find it. The power would be lost forever. All I had to do was haul it past the smugglers and drop it over the side.

Right. I rubbed my hands together.

A shout sounded from deck, and a moment later, the ship heeled to the side. I lost my balance, and fell, then shoved myself up.

My first thought was that something had hit the ship or

we had run into rocks. But then I heard the sound of sails coming down, and I realised: we had reached the harbour.

Too late. If I dropped this in the harbour, it would be recovered.

So get it to the ship's boat. Row it back out to sea. Tip it over the side and disappear.

"What the fuck do you think you're doing?"

I twisted to see the smugglers' leader in the doorway. Her pistol came up. I had no time to raise a shield. I threw myself to the side, and a bullet smacked into the planks, spraying splinters. I wrenched in raw magic and threw it as a solid block of force at her. Blood sprayed from her nose and mouth as she flew back.

Oh, I was in the shit now, I really was.

I glanced at the chest. There was no chance of lugging it out unnoticed. Depths, I wasn't even sure I could lift it.

Feet raced over the deck above, accompanied by more shouts.

Sink the ship? We were in the harbour. The ship would be raised, the chest found, the holy foot would be up for grabs again.

This whole thing was fucking absurd. I had to put an end to it, and I couldn't do that if they shot me.

I abandoned the chest, brought up my shield, and sprinted out into the main cabin, clutching my mage's rod tight. It was dark here after the blaze of light from the foot. Hammocks hanging from the ceiling like shrouds tangled around me. I pushed through with my shield, tumbling sleeping sailors to the floor.

A couple of smugglers appeared at the far end, guns already raised.

This is exactly what you wanted to avoid. As though this was ever going to end any other way. I smashed into them. The wall of magic flung them back.

Someone behind me shouted, and I swung the shield around in time for something to hit it.

The steps were just ahead. Up them, to the deck, then... what?

A pistol flashed from the left. A bullet hit the ceiling above me. I smelled smoke and sulphur.

Figure it out when you're out of here!

I threw a burning light behind me. Nothing that would hurt anyone – I didn't have the spare magic for that – but enough to temporarily blind them in the dark. Then I focused the shield above me, smashed it through the hatch, and came up the steps fast.

They were waiting for me on deck. I pulled the shield in tight and ducked to the side as the smugglers fired. Lead ricocheted from my shield.

I sprinted to the rail. It would take the smugglers time to reload, but holding the shield was a strain, particularly when I was trying to run and think at the same time.

We had passed the Dragon's Jaw on the right and the smaller sea wall on the left, and across the wide harbour I could see the outlines of ships tied up at the wharfs, the city lights glittering from the water, the bulk of the city against the dark sky.

Where was the ship's boat? It had been tied up ... somewhere. I looked desperately around as the smugglers advanced on me. I could fight, but I couldn't fight all of them forever. I was outnumbered.

I hated the fucking ocean.

I jumped over the side.

It wasn't exactly a dive. More a flailing, uncontrolled tumble. I hit the waves with a thump that almost knocked the breath from my body. I lost control of my shield on the way down, and I went under the water.

I panicked. The weight of my cloak, my trousers, my shoes, all pulled me down. Water clung to me like hands. I flailed, not knowing in the dark which way was up and which down. The ocean had taken Mica's dad, and now it wanted to take me. Salt water stung my eyes. I had to breathe. My chest was tight, my head dizzy, but there was no air, just blackness pressing around me.

No. I was a mage. I couldn't breathe underwater or fly or anything like that, but I could do *something*. I calmed myself, pushing away the increasing pressure in my throat and the pulse thumping in my head. The weight of the opal inside my shirt pulled down, trying to slip free and sink into the water. I drew in raw magic, focused it, and pushed myself in the opposite direction.

My head burst from the water. I gulped air, dashed water from my face, and kept the magic underneath me. I had hardly been below the surface at all. Slow, muted waves lifted and lowered me, and I let them, slowing my breath.

A shot sounded. Water sprayed up a foot from me. I

jerked around. The ship loomed over me, not ten feet away. Faces peered over the side, and another gun turned in my direction.

I swore, and pushed away with the magic, driving myself through the water.

At least we were inside the harbour. That was something. Here, I was protected from the heavy ocean waves and the tow of whatever currents were out there. *And the things that wait in the deep waters.*

Stop it! I didn't need monsters to scare me right now. I had a whole ship full of angry smugglers. When I glanced around, people were scrambling down to ship's boat.

It was at the back. Of course it was at the back.

I couldn't keep this magic up forever. The effort was too much. The docks still seemed impossibly far away across the enormous harbour. *Why couldn't they have waited until we were closer to shore?*

The Dragon's Jaw. There it was, a wall against the sea beyond. It wasn't so far. Less than a hundred yards. I could get there before the boat, climb up, and run. I angled towards it and shoved with magic. The strain made my bruises flare agonisingly and my head thump. But I was moving, and I wasn't drowning.

The magic lasted almost until I reached the Dragon's Jaw. Then it failed, my grip on the spell crumbling beneath the sapping weight of the water and my exhaustion. My head went under again, I swallowed salt water, choked, kicked and flailed, and my hand smashed into a rock. Skin split. Red pain flared through my knuckle. I swore, then found the rocks again. I hauled myself up, waist and legs still in the water, gasping for breath.

The small boat had launched, and it was rowing towards me, but the ship itself was continuing on its way into the harbour.

They would tie up somewhere – the shipyards, maybe, as planned – and then what? Try to get the foot out anyway and risk being seen? Stay put and try to capture or kill me? Risk bringing the purchaser to them?

No time to worry about it now.

My arms were shaking and weak as I dragged myself up the broken rocks. At least on this side of the Dragon's Jaw it wasn't a sheer drop. I ignored the shouts of the smugglers as I stumbled and scrambled my way up.

It was almost a mile along the Dragon's Jaw to reach Fishertown, then all the way across Agatos to reach the Ash Guard fortress. With clear streets and feeling fresh, maybe I could run it in half an hour, forty-five minutes. Right now, making it at all would be an achievement. Either way, the smugglers' ship would easily beat me to its mooring.

A hopeful shot from the approaching boat set me into a shambling run.

Mages weren't designed for fighting or athletic pursuits. Magic made too easy an alternative to most physical work. Your average mage had more in common with uncooked dough than with the smugglers pursuing me.

But I had some advantages. I had grown up in the Warrens, where running and fighting were a necessary part of life for kids, and my job seemed to involve me tramping back and forth across the city most days. I hadn't had the luxury to get lazy and unfit. Mages, too, sustained ourselves through the unconscious conversion of raw magic. At a push, a powerful enough mage could go without food or water for weeks. I wasn't in that class, but it was enough to keep me going and keep me ahead of my pursuers. I staggered along the Dragon's Jaw like a drunk being pursued by a dog, my mage's rod slapping painfully against my leg.

It was still the deep hours of the night. Ice-bright stars punctured a dead, black sky. There was no one around. Maybe guards in the small fort at the end of the Dragon's Jaw. But if I got them involved, there would be questions, statements to be taken, long explanations demanded. I didn't have time for that. At least with the distance between us and my wildly erratic gait, the smugglers weren't wasting time taking shots at me. If I could reach the city, maybe I could lose them in the alleys and back streets.

My legs felt like they were on fire. My lungs were raw.

Yeah? And how are you going to feel when you're full of bullets?

I pushed myself on.

My safest option would be to go to ground in Fishertown or the Grey City, or up in the Stacks. They wouldn't find me there. Someone would sell me out eventually, but not any time soon, if I was clever. But then the smugglers would have time to offload or hide the holy foot, and I would have nothing on them.

And while we were on the subject of dead gods' severed feet, this had to belong to Ethys, didn't it? That was why the raw magic was going mad in his temple. All it took was a chunk of the dead god to draw close. Maybe if I dealt with the dead god's foot, that would solve Dumonoc's problem, too. *Not that he'll thank you, the wanker.*

The end of the Dragon's Jaw was in sight, finally, the fort resolving itself against the blackness of the mountains beyond. The smugglers must have realised they were losing me. Footfalls rang louder. I grimaced and sped up. I was going to need new legs after this, even if they didn't capture and kneecap me.

I cleared the small fortress ahead of the smugglers and cut abruptly left into the tight, close streets of Fishertown. It stank of fish here, of course, gutted and their entrails thrown onto the rocky shore for the crabs, gulls, and tide. Gentle waves shushed and dragged over stones. Nets and floats hung suspended across alleys and courtyards. Boats hauled in for repair lay like dark mounds.

I hadn't been here in a long time, but I knew this place. Mica's dad had sometimes taken me out on his fishing boat from here, even after he had come to live with my mother in the Warrens. Before he had drowned and she had become the Countess, I had helped him drag his boat up over those stones, fasten it to the ropes that ran down the shore, lug out baskets of fish and crabs and lobsters. I remembered my way through the maze like I walked it every day. It was imprinted on me, even though I had only been here a few dozen times. Things stuck when you were a kid, and this wasn't like the ever-changing Warrens. Fishertown was old and as unchanging and solid as the mountains.

I kept running. The smugglers would have to divert around if they wanted to avoid confrontation. Either because I was running too fast, because of my black cloak, or because I was still recognised here, no one stopped me, but I felt eyes on me.

By the time I reached the Wet Bridge, the smugglers were no longer in sight. I slowed to regain my breath. I would have to avoid Dockside – that was the smugglers' territory – and cut through the Middle City, and I should keep away from Long Step Avenue and other major roads, too. If I had been the leader of the smugglers, I would have sent people out looking for me the moment they docked, to make sure I didn't do anything to fuck up their plans.

I was absolutely going to fuck up their plans.

No one was around as I crossed the Wet Bridge. The dark, flowing water was high beneath the bridge, the clustered houses on both banks dark. I hurried across, then took a sharp turn north to disappear into the back streets of the Grey City.

CHAPTER FOURTEEN

It took longer than I wanted to cross the Grey City and the Middle City. The ship would have docked long ago. I had to assume they hadn't already moved Ethys's foot. They wouldn't risk it unless they really had to. Any watching mage would know, and they *would* be watching the port.

The city was beginning to wake as I crept across it. It was still long before dawn, but the first servants and market traders were emerging. I wasn't used to being up at this time, and there was a certain peaceful quiet to the waking city. I might have appreciated it if I hadn't been worried about being murdered by angry smugglers.

The Ash Guard fortress was pressed against and burrowed into Giuffria's Spear. It loomed above the darkened houses from several streets away.

I had seen no signs of the smugglers since losing them

at Fishertown, but I couldn't believe they had just given up. I would be exposed for the first time crossing that plaza in front of the fortress. The leader of the smugglers was clearly smart. She must guess I would attempt to come here. Would they really try something in full sight of the Ash Guard? Maybe. The Guard only intervened in magical matters. If they saw me being gunned down or mobbed outside their building, would they step in if there was no magic involved? I hoped so, but relying on that and relying on them being fast enough felt too much like dangling my balls over a pit of snakes and hoping they wouldn't bite.

Approach from an alley. Put up a shield. Run.

My best bet would be to cut to the north, then double back through the alley that ran behind Somun's Bakery. The early shift would be there, baking the day's goods. Maybe those potential witnesses would be enough to deter the smugglers. Heart thumping like a landslide, I crossed the street I was on, heading for an intersecting alley.

A shot rang out, smacking off the cobbles. I ducked, involuntarily, then threw myself back, just as a second shot sounded.

Fuck! Where had those come from?

I pressed myself into a doorway. They weren't waiting for me to reach the plaza, but now they would all know I was near.

How many more of them were hiding, waiting, guns ready? I couldn't keep a shield up in every direction all the time, not reliably. I couldn't cover every alley, every doorway, every window, every rooftop.

I swore, then backed carefully away, shield between me and the end of the street. The moment I could, I slipped into a narrow cross street and ran.

Benny would have found a way over the roofs or down through the sewers. Sereh would have disappeared into the shadows. What did I have?

I slowed at the end of the street and ducked my head around the corner. Something flashed a block up, followed by the sound again of a shot. I jerked back. Shouts came from down the street.

There were too many of them in that gang for me to handle like this. Put them all in a locked room without their guns... But I wasn't getting past them here.

So maybe I needed to bring the Ash Guard here, to me. My *fucksthat* spell would do the job. It would bring people running from all around. I gathered raw magic and focused.

Another shot rang out, this time behind me. It hit the wall by my head, sending shards of stone spinning away. One lodged in my cheek. I yelled in pain.

Three figures appeared at the far end of the street I had fled down. One of them was waving, beckoning someone else out of sight. The others raised their guns. I dropped the *fucksthat* uncast and threw up my shield. *Just get out of here. Think again.* I ran, back through the Middle City, away from the Ash Guard fortress and the security of Captain Gale and her squad.

Now what? Shouts followed from behind, calling from

street to street, herding me away from where I needed to be.

The Penitent's Ear market came into sight, stalls being set up and goods being laid out after the few hours of night quiet. The market was already too busy. A stray shot could kill someone. I ran along the side, hugging the buildings. Ahead of me, the Royal Highway cut down through the city, from the north to the docks. The Temple of Ethys wouldn't be far, and with the dead god's foot so close, it would be blazing with raw magic. If I'd been a better mage, I could have used that power to royally fuck up the smugglers. If I'd been a better mage, I would never have been in this situation. That power was useless to me. But it would be overflowing, emerging into Dumonoc's bar.

And suddenly I knew what I had to do.

The smugglers hadn't stopped hunting me. They had been driving me further and further from the Ash Guard fortress, cutting off all my possible routes.

For what I was about to do, I needed time and quiet. That meant I had to lose the bastards.

I'd made several abortive attempts to find a way back to the Ash Guard, only to see them blocked, and I had become desperate. Let the smugglers see that desperation. Let them think I was making a final, all-in attempt to burst through.

The Penitent's Ear was the wrong place to do this. There were too many bystanders.

I darted up a street that led north, away from the

market. They would see me, follow me, warn their fellow smugglers on the next street that I was coming.

I was relying on that. I didn't expect to escape like this.

I drew in raw magic as I jogged over the cobbles, pulling it into me and holding it. The pressure made the deep cut on my cheek burn and my bruises throb.

There was no point going full *fucksthat* here. I didn't need them to think a fiend was clambering its way out of the Depths, and I was going to need some of my power to maintain a shield once the shooting started. But I did want them to notice me, and I reckoned I could modify the *fucksthat* to help.

I reached the end of the street, where it met Long Step Avenue, just as the first of my pursuers appeared behind me. Shouts sounded, followed by answering shouts from Long Step Avenue itself.

All right, boys and girls. Here we go.

I sucked in more raw magic, surrounded myself in a shield, and ran out into the street, heading directly for the line of smugglers who were advancing towards me a hundred yards ahead. I didn't have to fake a scream. Channelling this much magic felt like I was hammering nails into my bones and tearing fishhooks through my flesh.

I wasn't done yet.

You want me? You've got me. I detonated the modified *fucksthat* as I ran. Light erupted from me, blazing in a rainbow of colours. A phantom wind threw dust and scraps of trash into the air and rattled shutters. Strange shrieks and howls echoed between the buildings.

The smugglers ahead stumbled to a stop. I didn't blame them. It was fucking terrifying. A gun came up. I saw the powder ignite in a flash, but I didn't hear the shot over the unearthly sounds I had conjured. The bullet rebounded from my shield. A lucky, panicked shot. Lucky for me, too, that my shield was still holding.

I staggered, missing my footing. My body felt like it was burning, and blood dripped from my nose.

The smugglers retreated a step, then two. If they had realised that if I did reach them I would be as much use as a squid in a high-jump contest, they might have stood their ground.

I had no intention of reaching them.

Shots sounded behind, too, as the pursuing smugglers emerged.

This was what I had been waiting for.

I let the rest of the spell drop – I even let the shield drop – and fed all the power I could channel into light, so that I blazed brighter than the summer sun, blinding anyone looking towards me. As I did, I dived to the side, letting the blazing light continue down the street.

I rolled into the entrance of an alley, pulled the hood of my mage's cloak over my head, and slid into cover. I had never figured out how to disappear into shadows like Sereh could. She didn't use magic, and I'd had no luck duplicating the effect. But with the blinding light apparently sprinting down the street, no one would see a dark lump in a dark alley.

Casting a spell at a distance was one of the trickier feats

a mage could attempt, and most mages never mastered it. To cast magic, a mage had to draw in raw magic, change it into whatever structure they needed, and release it. Causing that magic to release at a distance was something I had taught myself to do as part of the *fucksthat*. I could hold it for a good couple of hundred yards if I focused. I didn't know how long it would last when I was lying battered and exhausted in a filthy alley.

I concentrated on the light, keeping it moving forward, ignoring my stolen opal digging into my ribs. A moment later, several figures raced past in pursuit of the fading light. I heard shots, but there was nothing out there for them to hit except each other. I gave it a few more seconds, checked the opal was still firmly tucked against my bruised side, then, before my grip on the magic could slip, I got to my feet and stumbled away, heading for the Grey City and Dumonoc's unwelcoming bar.

CHAPTER FIFTEEN

I WASN'T STUPID. I KNEW THE SMUGGLERS CHASING ME weren't the only smugglers out there. They were a big gang, but this was an even bigger city, and if they were focused on the Ash Guard fortress, they couldn't cover everywhere else. I crossed the Royal Highway in a black-cloaked scuttle and disappeared into the Grey City.

Dumonoc's wasn't far from here. A couple of streets east and a few more north. Keeping to the narrower, darker ways and avoiding the open plazas that characterised this part of Agatos, I made my way through the slowly waking Grey City. I knew this area well – I had lived here for five years – and it wasn't the first time I had gone skulking around.

I was right about the smugglers. They were here, but not in numbers. I saw one a way down Long Step Avenue, where it met the Tide Bridge, and another in a corner of

Feldspar Plaza, where I used to live. I thought these were the ones who had chased me down the Dragon's Jaw. That meant there were four more around here. Four I could handle if I had to, as long as they didn't catch me by surprise.

I angled away from my former home and took a sharp left to the small plaza in front of Dumonoc's bar.

There were two smugglers there, both holding guns, appearing to walk patrol.

This was more like it. If I could get a bit closer, I could jam their guns before they could fire, then knock them out with magic. Drag them into an alley where they wouldn't be found for hours.

I waited until they were heading away from me, then ran lightly across the empty plaza, magic held ready. They were chatting, tired, and it was nearly dawn. They weren't paying attention. I clutched my mage's rod in one hand in case I had to hit someone and shaped my spell.

This wasn't a blast of force to knock them flying. It was fine, careful work. All I wanted to do was to jam the hammers on their flintlocks. If the hammers couldn't fall, the flints wouldn't hit the steels, sparks wouldn't fly, there would be no ignited gunpowder and no bullets lodging themselves in the eye of an underappreciated mage. The problem was the hammers were small, the smugglers were swinging around their guns around like priests with incense, and the plaza was still deep in gloom.

Fine, detailed work had always been my strength as a mage.

I let my breath settle, prepared to release the spell—

A clattering rush on the paving stones behind me made me spin, mage's rod already coming up.

There was no smuggler there, no knife or cosh swinging for my head. In their place was an explosion of excited barking and leaping. I just had time to mutter, "What the fuck?" before I remembered the smugglers and dropped, throwing a shield over me and Mr. Inles's bloody dog.

The dog looked delighted. The smugglers less so. They raised their guns and fired. Shots bounced from my shield.

"I thought I bought you a leash," I muttered as I pushed myself up. The dog wagged its tail in response.

The thing about guns was that you never wanted to hang about, even as a mage. It took a highly-trained person maybe twenty seconds to reload, fifteen if they cut corners. I released my shield, gathered my power, and rushed them.

The smugglers were no fools. They dropped their firearms and drew knives.

I wasn't about to let this become a fair fight. I threw force at them, knocking them from their feet, and before they could recover, I was on them.

I swung my rod down, catching the first clean on his temple with the obsidian chunk embedded in the end.

The second slashed his knife at my legs. I leapt back, then hammered him again with magic. His head bounced from the stone, and I made sure he stayed down with another smack of my rod. I wasn't in the mood to pull the blow.

Mr. Inles's dog bounced around me, barking happily.

"I'm not chasing you this time," I told it. "Bugger off home."

From somewhere not too far away, a shout sounded, then an answering call a few streets further.

Bannaur's balls! They had heard the shots. No time to hide the bodies now. I took off at a run for Dumonoc's. I leapt down the steps, followed by the delighted dog, and hammered on the door.

No answer.

I hammered louder, pumping the sound with magic so it would thunder around the bar like cannons letting loose. I could trip the lock, but I knew Dumonoc kept the door barred, and I didn't want to break it down. I might need this door.

"All right. All fucking right," Dumonoc's voice called from inside. "Fucking arsehole."

A moment later, the door swung open. Dumonoc stared up at me. "You." He tried to close the door. I leaned on it, forcing it open.

"You want rid of that curse once and for all? Because it's now or never." Quite literally if the smugglers got me.

Dumonoc stared at me for a too-long moment. My back crawled at the thought of smugglers converging on me while I stood here in a glowering contest with bloody Dumonoc.

He threw open the door with a loud, "Fuck."

I stepped through, and Mr. Inles's dog followed.

"No dogs," Dumonoc said. The dog and I ignored him.

The place was trashed. The stink of sour wine and rotting food filled the air. The furniture had broken and crumbled. Decayed sawdust littered the floor.

The Jaunt's Ghost had been busy.

"Bit shitting late," Dumonoc said.

"It could still get worse." The timbers of the ceiling and walls were intact, and the bar itself was only beginning to slump. When I unfocused my eyes, I saw the tendrils of the Jaunt's Ghost spreading across the whole space, reaching for the walls and ceiling. Some were even tangling in Dumonoc's clothes. I really didn't want to be here when the Jaunt's Ghost started to consume those. Raw magic welled up from the floor in a dozen places, like as many bubbling hot springs, and the Jaunt's Ghost was focused on that, consuming it and growing. When the raw magic receded, the main entity would go dormant again, and its remaining tendrils would rip the raw magic from anything that had ever been living here, from the remnants of food and drink to the wood of the structure and our clothes.

"Lock the door," I told Dumonoc. "We might be having guests."

"You know this is a fucking drinking establishment, right?" Dumonoc muttered as he slid the wooden bar back in place.

"And I know you hate having customers. Trust me, you'll hate these ones even more."

He muttered something else, but I deliberately didn't hear.

The door was sturdy, but it wouldn't hold forever. I

added a magical lock to slow them down, then turned back to the chaos of the bar.

At least I'd had a chance to practice this on the smuggler's ship. Kind of.

I crossed to where the largest upwelling of raw magic emerged from the floor. The Jaunt's Ghost was strong here, covering the raw magic with a net of tendrils and consuming it before it could spread.

I pulled the opal from inside my shirt. It was wet, dirty, and it was a miracle that it was still intact. I felt instant empathy.

Now all I had to do was get to the raw magic.

I shaped a delicate blade of power and sliced through the tendrils. They snapped back, as though burned, and raw magic jetted up, like water from a burst pipe. I grabbed it, pulled it towards me as if I were preparing a spell, then at the last moment, directed it towards the opal in my hand.

I saw raw magic settle in there, but not enough. Most of it rushed past.

I swore.

All right. Try a different way.

I took hold of the raw magic again and brought it towards the opal, swirling it around the gem, ever closer, like water circling a drainpipe, then in. My head wanted to explode. Blood ran from my nose, over my lips, and dripped from my chin.

Abruptly, the raw magic stopped. I blinked. New tendrils had formed over the upwelling, smothering it.

This was harder than I'd imagined. The opal was

glowing a pale green in my magical vision. It was working, but it was nowhere near enough.

A tendril reached for the opal. I sliced it away. *Not yet.*

Try again. Ignoring my pulsing headache, I sliced away the net covering the upwelling and spiralled more power into the opal.

Hammering sounded from the door.

"Don't answer that!" I gasped, fighting my splitting head.

"What the fuck have you bought to my door, Thorn?"

I didn't answer. The Jaunt's Ghost's tendrils were growing back fast, trying to encompass the upwelling of magic again and reaching for the opal.

The more raw magic it consumed, the faster the Jaunt's Ghost grew and the stronger the tendrils became. I felt like a kid trying to hold back the tide with a barrier of beach pebbles.

The hammering outside grew louder, and shouts sounded.

"I'm opening the door before they smash it down." Dumonoc strode across the bar.

I spared an ounce of magic to snatch his legs out from under him. He hit the floor hard.

The distraction was enough for me to lose control. The Jaunt's Ghost's tendrils whipped out and around the upwelling, enclosing it and cutting it off in less than a second. I staggered back, fighting away the tendrils reaching for the opal.

Not yet!

The Jaunt's Ghost had entirely capped the upwellings of raw magic now, sealing them so completely that none of the raw magic was making it into the bar. I wondered if it would chase the magic back to its source in the Temple of Ethys.

Dumonoc came to his feet, spitting curses and blood from his broken lips. "Get the fuck out of my bar!"

My head was ready to burst. Every knock, bruise, and cut on my body burned like I was being stabbed with red hot knives. I wasn't in the mood to back down. I bullied up to him, topping him by a full head.

"You have two choices. You can open that door, and within an hour your whole fucking bar will be rubble, or you can *sit the fuck down and shut the fuck up.*"

Something about me – maybe it was the blood or the fury or the solid mage's rod I jammed towards him with my spare hand – made him back away.

"You're fucking barred," he muttered. "You're fucking barred ten times over."

I turned back to the room. My opal was incandescent with raw magic, but it still wasn't enough. Gritting my teeth, I reached out and began severing the tendrils over the upwelling again.

I managed to keep going for another minute before I couldn't force any more raw magic into the opal and until I couldn't fight the tendrils off the upwelling. Maybe Mica or the blessed Countess could have kept going, but I was done. My shirt was soaked with blood, and I could barely stand. The opal raged with a green light in my magical vision that was hard to look at.

The smugglers – I assumed it was the smugglers, unless someone really hated Dumonoc's wine – had brought something heavy against the door, and the wood was splintering.

Before the smugglers had grabbed me, I'd hoped to have more time to deal with Dumonoc's problem. I'd hoped to wait until the raw magic drained away and the Jaunt's Ghost became dormant again. With Ethys's severed foot having reached the city, I wondered if it ever would again. Somehow, I had to make the Jaunt's Ghost release all the other sources of raw magic and attract it to the opal.

The creature was everywhere. Its tendrils might be clustered around the upwellings of magic, but they had also spread throughout the bar, even through the walls and the ceiling, searching for more sources of raw magic to consume.

It's still a creature. A magical entity, perhaps, but it had a centre, a place from where all the tendrils were emanating.

I focused, still slapping away the tendrils trying to reach my opal.

Not yet.

There. Under the remains of a table. That was where the Jaunt's Ghost itself was waiting. I picked my way across the bar, drawing in as much raw magic as I could, then kicked away the remnants of the table and stood right in the middle of the thing. It was an odd sensation. My magical sight was telling me I was standing in a seemingly-dense sea-blue cluster of magic. But there was nothing physically there to touch.

Tendrils lashed for the opal, in a frenzy now that it was close.

Hold on. Hold on.

I shaped my magic into a long blade, extended it away from me – *Here we go* – and slashed in a wide circle around the Jaunt's Ghost, severing every tendril. At the same time, I dropped my defence of the opal. Tendrils snatched it, and the Jaunt's Ghost seemed to lunge, wrapping itself around the opal.

It was so fast, I almost couldn't react. More tendrils snapped out, reaching again for the upwellings of raw magic that were erupting like a cluster of overexcited volcanos into the bar. I shoved the raw magic away from the opal. With nothing to grab hold of, the tendrils waved helplessly in the air.

The Jaunt's Ghost was hungry. Within seconds, it had consumed all the raw magic I had stored in the opal. As I watched, it faded, going dormant again.

I had done it. I had it. I genuinely hadn't thought this would work.

As long as I didn't expose the Jaunt's Ghost to any powerful sources of raw magic, it would stay dormant. Which was why standing in the middle of this bar was a Depths-cursed stupid idea.

A splintering crash against the door snatched me back to reality.

I was soaked in sweat and blood and hardly standing,

still having to hold back a tidal wave of raw magic, and that door was about to break.

I spun towards Dumonoc, who had retreated behind his bar to glower at me. I wondered what all this must look like without magical vision. I must look a right twat, prancing about, muttering, and waving my hands in the air.

"Do you have a back door?" I demanded.

He gave me a flat look. "Have you seen a back door?"

"How about through your kitchen?"

"That's private."

I took a step towards him. "Where does it lead?"

"Upstairs." The reluctance in his voice was thick. "Then out front."

"No back way?"

"No. No pissing back way."

So, fight my way out or—

The door smashed off its hinges, the wooden bar holding it splitting in two. The lock spun across the floor. Smugglers poured in, guns levelled.

I slipped the opal inside my shirt and held up my hands. "I surrender."

As the smugglers forced me out the door, I turned back to Dumonoc. "Look after my dog, because if you don't, I'm not going to be happy when I get back."

CHAPTER SIXTEEN

THEY HUSTLED ME ACROSS AGATOS IN THE PALE DAWN LIGHT, keeping to the narrow, darker ways. The large, heavily armed group was enough to send any passing dockworkers and sailors scuttling for cover.

I didn't know if I would be coming back from this. I felt absurdly guilty that I hadn't been able to return Mr. Inles's dog to him. As though it wouldn't have escaped again by tomorrow. At least the smugglers hadn't shot me down right away. That had to be a good sign, didn't it? They still needed me.

They'll shoot you right after.

I didn't plan on giving them the chance.

At first, I thought they were taking me to their new base in the dockside tavern, but they only gathered a few more of their number before carrying on. There had to be forty or fifty of them accompanying me now, both in a tight group and in a couple of loose rings.

This has to be all of them.

Enough for the ships they ran and to protect their stashes.

They weren't taking any chances this time.

Bad move.

By the time we reached the dockyards, the tops of the western mountains were glowing pastel with the morning light, the waves on the water of Erastes Bay glittered in silver threads, and the heat of the summer day was already creeping into the air.

Another hour and the smugglers might have had to go to ground.

Too late for that.

No one tried to stop us at the entrance to the dockyard. I wondered if anyone had seen me being led here. The Wren undoubtedly had watchers, but the smugglers had paid him off, as every criminal in the lower city did, and if he didn't know about the dead god's foot, he wouldn't interfere. The Wren, in turn paid the Watch to turn a blind eye. It was a neat, peaceful arrangement until you were kidnapped by smugglers and nobody saw a thing.

The smugglers' ship was tied up against the dockyard quay, as though waiting to be hauled in for repair. The customs officers would arrive to inspect it soon. I wondered what would happen if they did arrive. With such a valuable cargo, would they be met with guns, or would the smugglers hope to keep it concealed?

The question was moot. I had the feeling they weren't intending to hang around, and I would be helping them smuggle this out of here before the customs agents had finished their breakfasts.

Or so they thought. I had other ideas.

A pistol in the back sent me up the gangplank, then down into the bowels of the ship. Eyes watched me from the shadows. I heard smugglers spread out across the deck. Another couple of dozen followed me down, guns held ready. Even the Wren would have been flattered by these precautions. Right before he turned them into paste.

I didn't have the Wren's power, but I did have a plan, and that had to be better, right?

The smuggler behind prodded me on.

The chest sat where I had left it, in the cabin at the back of the ship. The smugglers gathered around the chest and behind me. No one had lowered their gun.

The smugglers' leader strode to stand beside the chest. Her eyes were flat, and her fists opened and closed. Her lips and nose were swollen and red from where I had smashed her with magic. It hadn't improved her mood. "You've caused us a lot of trouble."

I gestured down at my sweat- and bloodstained shirt. "It hasn't exactly been a party on my end, either."

That earned me a jab in the kidney from one of her flunkies. I grunted.

"We're taking this out now. Do your job, hide the item from prying eyes, and we might all get out of this. Fail..."

Her hand dropped to the knife on her belt. "I'll cut out your eyes myself, and I hope you fucking scream."

Nice.

I slowed my heartbeat, let my shoulders relax, and sucked in raw magic.

I would have only one chance at this.

I crafted a spell, then reached out with it and flipped open the lids of the chest, both the apple tree wood and the volcanic glass.

Raw magic exploded from it, a thousand times brighter than the magic I had managed to trap in the opal. The upwellings in Dumonoc's bar had been shadows compared to this.

The dormant Jaunt's Ghost woke. Tendrils burst from it, flailing in every direction, engulfing the dead god's foot and stabbing outwards, through the hull and the walls and the deck above. In the time it took me to blink, the overwhelming raw magic of Ethys's severed foot caused the Jaunt's Ghost to grow to a monstrous size. It was what I had been planning, but even so, the sheer speed and scale shocked me.

None of the smugglers were mages. None of them were seeing this.

"What the fuck are you doing?" the smugglers' leader demanded. She slammed the chest shut.

Bad, bad mistake.

Cut off from Ethys's foot, the Ghost's tendrils ripped the raw magic from everything they touched.

The ship crumpled like paper in a fist. The hull caved

in, ropes parted, and cloth shredded. I just had time to wrap myself in a shield before the water smashed in like the clap of a giant's hands. The mast above fell, bringing down the spars, the rigging, and the furled sails into the churning chaos of water and shredded planks. I was tossed like a rag in a hurricane, pulled down, wrenched to the side, and thrown up, colliding with stone and sharp wood. Only my shield kept me safe.

Water churned like a cauldron. Fragments of wreckage and torn bodies swirled past me. Mud and debris were ripped from the bed of the harbour. My shield was battered with steam-hammer blows. Despite my best efforts, air leaked out, and the shield tightened around me.

I fought against the water, pushing up with magic, unable to see anything, my ears nearly deaf from the rage of destruction.

Then it was gone. I burst out of the water, my shield finally failing. Battered and exhausted, I hauled myself out.

The Jaunt's Ghost had caused more damage than I could have imagined. The ship was gone completely, of course, but part of the quayside had been ripped away, too. Waves still rebounded across the harbour. Broken bodies of smugglers floated among decayed fragments of planks. Gulls screamed above. The very air seemed shocked.

I turned my eyes away from what I had done and waited on the remains of the dockyard quay until the Ash Guard finally arrived.

Better late than never.

~

Captain Gale was not impressed as she surveyed the destruction around me. "What? Decided to start early?"

Heat haze shivered above the broken stone of the quay. "Wasn't exactly my idea." I nodded towards the muddy water. "There's a dead god's foot down there. Ethys, I think. You'll find it inside a volcanic glass chest inside one made of apple tree wood. You might want to retrieve it before the city's mages figure it out and get to it first."

I told her what had happened – the edited version – and when I was finished, she shook her head.

"That's a real talent you've got there, Nik. And not a good one. Why does this stuff not happen to anyone else?"

I shrugged. "Unlucky, I guess."

"Yeah, I don't think it's that."

I pushed painfully to my feet. Every part of my body hurt, and I looked shit. "Are we done? Because I'm..." I gestured down to my bloodstained, torn shirt.

"Yeah. Go home. Get some rest." She met my eyes. It made me shiver. I wasn't quite sure why. "There are going to be more questions. That's a lot of dead bodies out there, even for you."

"Fine." I winced as I straightened. "But I'm going to sleep for a long time first." I made to leave, then paused. "Oh, and one more thing. I lost my mage's rod down there. If you come across it, I could really do with getting it back." That thing had been expensive, and it had split a good number of deserving heads in its time. I would hate to have to replace it.

Her eyebrows shot up. "That's what you call it? Your 'mage's rod'? That's a little ... I want to say, 'on the nose', but then I really don't want to say that."

"Good night, Meroi," I said as I turned away.

She didn't object to me using her given name. I must have done something right. That was enough for me, for now.

I MUST HAVE SLEPT ALL DAY AND THROUGH THE NIGHT, because when I woke it was dawn again. I was hungry, thirsty, and still exhausted, but most of my injuries had healed well enough. I found some almost-clean clothes and headed out.

The crowds outside the Temple of Ethys had dispersed. Only a few hangdog priests loitered outside, calling to passers-by. I almost felt sorry for them – almost. Agatos moved on quickly. One moment you were the exciting new thing, the next, forgotten. I peered through the temple door. The blindingly intense raw magic had gone, leaving only the thin green mist that permeated the city. Captain Gale must have retrieved the god's foot and buried it in Ash.

The statue of Ethys had fallen from where it had floated above the altar and cracked. I would have liked to say that its foot had broken off, but reality didn't do poetic.

I turned away from the disconsolate priests and their empty, gilded temple and went to retrieve Mr. Inles's dog from Dumonoc. At least it would be pleased to see me.

- End -

Mennik Thorn will return in the final book, Legacy of a Hated God, in 2023.

LEGACY OF A HATED GOD

THE FINAL MENNIK THORN NOVEL.

Nik Thorn should know better than to get involved with gods.

But when a priest of a hated god asks Nik to save his life, Nik can hardly refuse, particularly when the priest knows exactly how, where, when, and why he is going to be killed. How hard can it be?

If only that was Nik's only problem, because a god has been murdered, the city's high mages are about to go to war, and fury is rising in the streets.

Agatos will burn.

Order now.

APPENDIX 1: THE REGION OF AGATOS

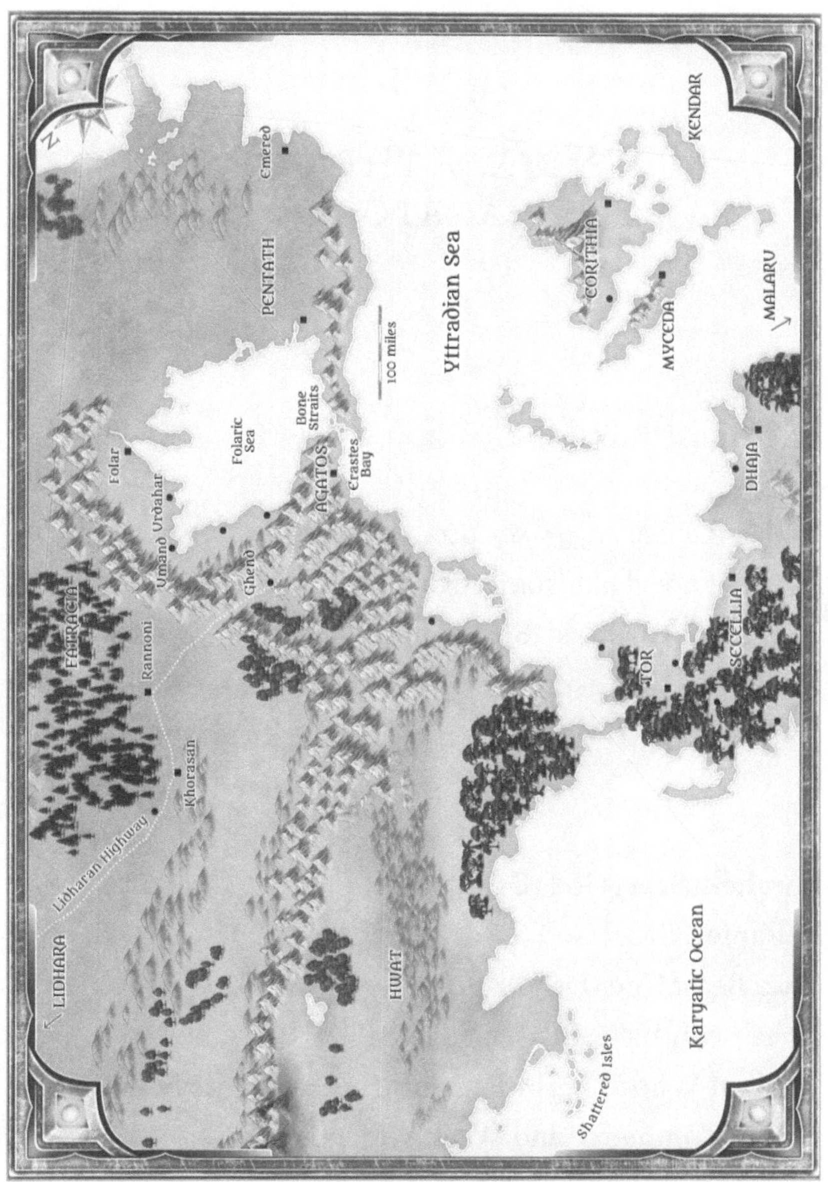

See larger map: patricksamphire.com/agatos-region

APPENDIX 2: THE GODS OF AGATOS

THERE HAVE BEEN MANY GODS WORSHIPPED IN AGATOS. SOME of these are dead, some living, and some whose status is pointlessly disputed. Some, although not all, are associated with particular aspects or locations. Here are some of the gods you may encounter in the Mennik Thorn books.

Karchek: Beast God (Dead)
Bellamer: Beast God (Dead)
Mur: Beast God (Dead)
Ah'té / Nimha'té: Beast God (Dead)
Gwillan-Whose-Light-Falls-on-the-Few-Not-the-Many: God of Commerce and Wealth (Living)
Belethea: Goddess of Bees (Dead)
The Lady of the Grove: Patron God of the Warrens (Living)
Sharshak: Sun God (Dead)

Mara: Sky God (Living)
Kethcal: Sky God (Dead)
Talifa: Mycedan God (Dead)
Sien, the Lady of Dreams Descending: Patron Goddess of Eras / Agatos (Dead)
Stypar: Sea God (Living)
Yttra: Sea God (Living)
Denna: Lord of the Depths (Living)
Cepra: God of Death (Living, ironically)
Tulbek the Old: Fatracian God (Dead)
The Nameless God / the Hated God: Brythanii God (Living)
Lord Ensio: God of Luck (Living)
Oleos: Eel God (Dead)
Shapray: God of Arbitrary Decisions and Unjustifiable Demands
Chaerd the Unkind: God of Missed Opportunities
Niarret / Enhuin / Enabgal, the Watcher in the Dark: God of Nightmares, Sea God (Living)
Ethys: War God of Melaru (Dead)
Bannaur (Disputed)
Narth the Sleeping (Disputed)
Putchek (Living)
Felen (Dead)

APPENDIX 3: CURRENCY

Currency in Agatos is actually quite simple, consisting of four basic units: the piece, the oar, the shield, and the crown. However, the residents of Agatos don't make anything easy, so I am including a guide to help you follow the ins-and-outs of money in Agatos.

Value

Piece (iron): comes in units of ½, 1, 2, 5.
Oar (copper): 1 oar = 10 pieces
Shield (silver): 1 shield = 40 oars
Crown (gold): 1 crown = 12 shields

Slang Terms

½ piece: Cut, waste, splinter
1 piece: Penny
2 pieces: Pair
5 pieces: Hand
Oar: Sailor's hand, round
Shield: Watchman, silver
Crown: God, king, gold, bank

APPENDIX 4: MONTHS OF THE YEAR

1. Elletos
2. Mael
3. Unchera
4. Fichera
5. Missos
6. Eppos
7. Keratos
8. Thieth
9. Enetha
10. Irratos
11. Imminas
12. Coel
13. Andaros

KEEP IN TOUCH

Subscribe to my newsletter to get a free short story in the world of SHADOW OF A DEAD GOD and NECTAR FOR THE GOD, and to be the first to find out about future books: patricksamphire.com/newsletter/

You can find out about all my other books and stories at my website: patricksamphire.com

You can often find me on Twitter (twitter.com/patricksamphire) as well as on my Facebook page (facebook.com/patricksamphireauthor/).

A REQUEST

PLEASE REVIEW THIS BOOK!

Reviews help authors more than you probably imagine, and for independent authors, they are everything. It would mean an awful lot to me if you could leave a brief review - a sentence or two is perfect! - wherever you bought this book or on a service like Goodreads.

READ MORE

THE CASEBOOK OF HARRIET GEORGE

Mystery, murder, and adventure on Mars...

Mars in 1815 is a world of wonders, from the hanging ballrooms of Tharsis City to the air forests of Patagonian Mars, and from the depths of the Valles Marineris to the Great Wall of Cyclopia, beyond which dinosaurs still roam.

Join Harriet George and her hapless brother-in-law, Bertrand, as they solve mysteries and try to save their family from ruin.

Volume 1: The Dinosaur Hunters.

Volume 2: A Spy in the Deep.

Available in paperback and ebook.

ABOUT PATRICK SAMPHIRE

Patrick Samphire started writing when he was fourteen years old and thought it would be a good way of getting out of English lessons. It didn't work, but he kept on writing anyway.

He has lived in Zambia, Guyana, Austria, and England. He has been charged at by a buffalo and, once, when he sat on a camel, he cried. He was only a kid. Don't make this weird.

Patrick has worked as a teacher, an editor and publisher of physics journals, a marketing minion, and a pen pusher (real job!). Now, when he's not writing, he designs websites and book covers. He has a PhD in theoretical physics and never uses it, so that was a good use of four years.

Patrick now lives in Wales, U.K. with his wife, the awesome writer Stephanie Burgis, their two sons, and their cat, Pebbles. Right now, in Wales, it is almost certainly raining.

He has published almost twenty short stories and novellas in magazines and anthologies, including *Realms of Fantasy*, *Interzone*, *Strange Horizons*, and *The Year's Best*

Fantasy, as well as two novels for children, SECRETS OF THE DRAGON TOMB and THE EMPEROR OF MARS.

STRANGE CARGO is his third novel for adults. It is the sequel to SHADOW OF A DEAD GOD and NECTAR FOR THE GOD. The final book in the series is LEGACY OF A HATED GOD.

facebook.com/patricksamphireauthor
x.com/patricksamphire
instagram.com/patricksamphire

www.ingramcontent.com/pod-product-compliance
Lightning Source LLC
Chambersburg PA
CBHW020525310726
48979CB00014B/2210/J
* 9 7 8 1 7 3 9 1 1 7 6 0 3 *